F
HIC

Hicks, Clifford B.

The marvelous
inventions of Alvin
Fernald

FEB 28 '78	MAR. 7 DATE	MAR 19 '80	12
FEB 28 '78 12	MAR 7 12	MAR 19 '80 12	
JUL 3 SUN 12	MAY 4 '79 P.1	OCT 9 NAY 12	
78 12	79 12	APR 90 '8 78	
MAR 30 '78 12	SEP 18 '79 2	F	
APR 13 '78 12	79 3	MAY - 2 1983	
81 02 78 13	12		
29 12	JAN 16 '80 12		
MAY 3 '78 12	JAN 23 '80 12		
JUL 11 78 12	JAN 30 '80		
MAY 18 '78 12	FEB 13 '80 12		
JUL 23 78	FEB 20 '80 12		
	MAR 12 '80 12		

The Marvelous Inventions
of Alvin Fernald

The Marvelous Inventions of Alvin Fernald

CLIFFORD B. HICKS

Illustrated by Charles Geer

HOLT, RINEHART AND WINSTON

NEW YORK   CHICAGO   SAN FRANCISCO

F
Hic

PUBLISHED, JANUARY, 1960

8 9 10 11 12 13 14 15

Library of Congress Catalog Card Number 60-6055

ISBN: 0–03–089893–3

Printed in the United States of America

For Rae

mother of my own three Alvins

Contents

Chapter 1

ALVIN awoke with a start the instant the string jerked his big toe. Quickly, he reached down and turned off the alarm clock before his toe turned purple.

Each morning a jerk on his big toe woke up Alvin Fernald. Alvin was a Great Inventor, and the string was one of his inventions. It ran to an alarm clock which he had bolted to the foot of his bed. He had removed the alarm bell so it wouldn't wake his parents. When the alarm went off each morning it wound up a string which was tied to his big toe. Sometimes the toe became purple before he could turn off the alarm, but otherwise the Silent Waker Upper worked fine.

Alvin had to get up early each morning to deliver his papers. He received $2.26 a week for delivering the papers before seven o'clock, and he promptly spent it for springs, wire, bolts, radio tubes, washers, light bulbs, and old clocks for his inventions.

Alvin always considered himself a Great Inventor, capitalized. In fact, Alvin's mind always capitalized his great inventions. He thought of himself as another Thomas Alva Edison (though, to himself, he always said Thomas *Alvin* Edison). And, like all Great Inventors, Alvin's mind was continually working on some kind of a problem.

1

This particular morning his magnificent brain was working on the problem of the Sure Shot Paper Slinger. Would it work? The first real test would come this morning on the paper route. Alvin was so intent on the problem that he didn't notice anything wrong until he saw himself standing slantwise in the mirror. Then he discovered that he'd put on one shoe and one ice skate, which he'd been kicking around the closet floor since last winter.

Alvin was a short, freckle-faced twelve-year-old who didn't care much how he dressed, anyway. As a matter of fact, except for Sunday school, he hadn't had on his good pair of pants since the last day of school, and here it was the middle of the summer. Alvin hated to see the summer go by so fast because fall meant school, and schoolwork didn't leave him enough time to invent. He lived in Riverton, a middle-sized town in Indiana, and even the adults in town knew that Alvin was a Great Inventor.

They'd never forget the time, three years ago, when he "motorized" his sister's tricycle, put her on the seat and started the gasoline engine. She'd rolled down Hickory Street, gradually picking up speed, sailed around the corner into the business district, zoomed past the Cashway Hardware Store, crashed through the door of McAllister's Drug Store, and ended up in a heap beside the soda fountain. When Mr. McAllister picked her up to see if she was hurt, she ordered a chocolate sundae. Her trip made headlines in the local paper, and from that moment everyone in town knew that Alvin was a Great Inventor.

Alvin kicked the skate back into the closet, found his other shoe, and put it on. He had to struggle to pull on his pants because the pockets were so bulgy, but that was nothing unusual for Alvin's pockets. He put everything on the dresser, making a pile that included a screwdriver, knife, three pennies, a jelly sandwich left over from the previous afternoon, an old bike pedal, three keys that didn't fit anything, a chain of paper clips, and several bolts of various sizes. Everything went back into his pockets except the sandwich.

Alvin flipped the switch that turned on his Foolproof Burglar Alarm and slipped quietly out the door, closing it behind him. In the bathroom he washed his face and brushed his teeth.

At the top of the steps the Pest was waiting, fully

dressed, her football clutched in her arms. Actually, the Pest was Daphne, his little sister. But the Pest was what Alvin had called her as long as he could remember.

"You go back to bed," he whispered fiercely. "You're not supposed to get up when I do."

"I'm coming along, Alvin."

"No you're not. You're going back to bed. Now get out of my way. I have an important invention to try out."

He stepped around her and ran down the steps two at a time. As he held the front door so it wouldn't slam, she slipped out, her golden curls brushing his arm.

Daphne was only eight years old, and she was small for her age. She was as quick and graceful as a kitten, and she managed to pop up in the most unexpected places. Usually they were places where Alvin didn't want her to pop up. He was always complaining to his parents that she stuck the freckles on her turned-up nose into business where the freckles on her turned-up nose didn't belong.

Because she worshipped Alvin, Daphne wished she was a boy. Whenever her mother would let her, she dressed in Alvin's outgrown blue jeans. And, although she had a dozen dolls with complete outfits, she hid them away in her closet and insisted on carrying around an old football wherever she went.

"You go on back," Alvin insisted.

"I want to watch."

From years of experience Alvin knew that it was useless to argue with Daphne. He walked on out to the garage.

In the open door he paused a moment for a good look at his latest great invention. There it was, fastened to the rear wheel of his bike. Man, oh man, it looked good! Why, he'd probably make a million dollars on it, besides helping every paperboy in the world. It was a genuine, never-before-invented Sure Shot Paper Slinger.

The invention stood out on one side of the rear wheel. There were a lot of complicated parts, but mainly it was made of a broom handle, an inner tube rubber, two screen-door springs, and a tube made of cardboard that was big enough to hold a rolled-up paper. Two levers on the handlebars operated the invention.

"Oh, Alvin," said the Pest. "It's beautiful."

"May not work," he replied. "May not work at all. You never can tell about an invention until you test it."

"Test it." Daphne frequently repeated whatever she heard. "Oh, Alvin! it's so beautiful. Let's test it quick."

The Pest thought all his inventions were beautiful. All except the Foolproof Burglar Alarm which kept her from sneaking into his room.

As Alvin wheeled out the bicycle he saw Shoie trotting up the driveway.

"Hi!" said Shoie. "All ready to try it out?"

Shoie — his name was Wilfred Shoemaker, but all the kids called him Shoie — was Alvin's best friend. He was taller than Alvin and he could run lots faster and jump much higher. In fact, Shoie was considered the mightiest athlete in all of Roosevelt School.

"Hi, Shoie," said Alvin. "Let's go pick up the papers and try out this good ol' Sure Shot Paper Slinger."

With his left foot on the pedal, Alvin shoved off and started to swing his right foot up over the seat. Instead, he caught it in the Paper Slinger, lost his balance and crashed into Shoie. Immediately there was a tangle of arms, legs, and bike on the driveway.

The Pest looked down at them. "What did you do that for, Alvin?" she asked.

"Don't just lie there," Alvin shouted at Shoie. "Get off, so I can see whether or not we ruined the Paper Slinger!"

Apparently there was no damage to the invention.

"Come on. Help me get on the bike and I'll wait for you at the corner."

But the Mighty Athlete was so fast on his feet that he was balancing on his head on top of the pile of papers when Alvin came riding up. A moment later the Pest showed up, out of breath. Each morning the delivery truck dropped off a pile of papers on this corner, and it was Alvin's job to see that they were delivered. Usually Shoie came along just for the fun of it.

The boys rolled each paper into a tight bundle and dropped it into the wire basket in front of the handlebars. At last they were ready for the big test.

"Excuse me for asking," said Shoie, as he steadied Alvin on the seat, "but how come you made this Paper Slinger? Can't you throw them just as good with your arm, old bean?"

Alvin and Shoie always called each other "old bean" and "old man."

For a minute Alvin acted as though he wasn't even going to answer. Then he said in a disgusted tone, "It's plain to see that you'll never be an inventor. Anything that your arm can do, a machine can do better. Why, lots of times I throw papers on roofs and everywhere else, but I'll bet this Paper Slinger will throw them exactly the same place every time."

Alvin thought a minute. Then he added, "Besides, you don't know how sore my arm gets slinging these papers day after day." (Alvin knew this wasn't quite true. He'd never had a sore arm except the time he'd hurt it throwing a rock at the big old bull out on Maldowski's farm. And Shoie probably knew it, too, because Shoie usually slung just as many papers as he did.) "Just think of it. There are a million, maybe two million paperboys all over the United States. And every day every one of them gets a sore arm just from slinging papers. If they throw with both arms that's maybe four million sore arms every day. And if this invention works, there won't be a single sore arm on a paperboy anywhere."

"My brother's the best thinker in the whole world," said the Pest. No matter how Alvin treated her, she always stood up for him.

"Everybody quiet," said Alvin. "It's time for a scientific test."

With that he shoved off and started pedaling.

As he approached Mr. McRobert's house — the first house on his route — Alvin took one of the papers out of the basket, reached around and slipped it into the cardboard tube on the Paper Slinger. Then he grabbed the special cocking lever on the handlebars. He had to pull so hard to get it cocked that he almost crashed into the curb. Finally, he was ready for the big test.

Alvin could feel his heart beating faster as he came up to Mr. McRobert's house. It was the same feeling he always had when he was about to test a great invention.

He took a deep breath and reached for the special release trigger.

Just as he wheeled past the house he gave a quick jerk. The two springs slammed against the rear wheel of the bike, and for a moment Alvin thought he'd been hit by a truck. The instant before he crashed, he heard a whistling sound behind his ear. With the bike on top

of him, he twisted around and looked toward the house. High in the air, high above the peak of the roof, the paper unfolded with a snap and pages went fluttering in all directions.

By the time Shoie came running up, the morning paper was spread all over the top of Mr. McRobert's house.

Chapter 2

VISIT TO A HAUNTED HOUSE

"WOW!" shouted Shoie. "Boy, that was something! Did you see that paper fly? Let's do it again!"

"Didn't work right," mumbled Alvin, rubbing his leg. "Too much tension. I'll have to make an adjustment."

He scrambled to his feet. With the screwdriver from his pocket, he loosened the two screen-door springs, moved a bolt, and refastened the springs, looser this time.

"There," he said. "That ought to be just about right. Let's try it again, Shoie."

When Alvin had crashed, the papers had rolled into the street. The two boys reloaded them into the basket. Soon, Alvin was pedaling down the street again. He'd wasted a paper on Mr. McRobert's roof, and had left his only spare copy on the front steps. That meant he couldn't afford to ruin another one. He sure hoped the tension was right.

As he approached old Mr. Bugle's house he pulled the special cocking lever again. This time it wasn't so hard to pull, and he thought the tension might be about right.

He rode close to the curb. When he was exactly in front of the house, he jerked the special release trigger. There was a jar to the bike, but it didn't knock him over. He heard the whistling sound behind his ear, and looked back over his shoulder.

The paper sailed through the air and landed smack on the top step of old Mr. Bugle's front stoop.

"Perfect!" shouted Shoie, turning a handspring. "Alvin, you've made an invention that really works."

Alvin circled around and stopped. In the middle of his stomach was a warm feeling — the same kind of feeling he'd had when he got two A's on the same report card. In fact, he felt mighty good all over. Still, he didn't want Shoie to think he was overcome.

"Not bad," he admitted, "but it should have slung that paper about two feet farther. I'll adjust it better tomorrow." He paused a minute to impress Shoie. "Yep. I think this old Sure Shot Paper Slinger is going to work fine." Then, as an afterthought, "Maybe I'll try to get a patent on it this afternoon."

"Let's try it again, Alvin," begged Shoie.

Shoie helped him shove off again, then ran along the sidewalk while Alvin pedaled down the street. The next time Alvin tried the Paper Slinger, the paper whistled through the air and landed in the bushes at the side of the house. Alvin figured it was his fault; he'd pulled the special release trigger too soon. He circled around in the street while Shoie found the paper and dropped it on the porch.

But it wasn't long until Alvin was hitting the front steps almost every time. And each time a paper landed right on target, Shoie would do a handspring as he raced down the sidewalk and shout, "Atta boy, old bean! Atta boy!"

It was true, of course, that a paper knocked two roses off Mrs. Whittaker's favorite bush, and another hit the Kawolsky dog smack on the rear end. Alvin felt sorry about the two roses, but he couldn't feel sorry for the dog. Now, maybe it wouldn't nip his heels every morning as he rode past.

By the time he had delivered most of his papers, Alvin knew he had a truly great invention. In front of Shoie he had pretended to know something about getting a patent, but he really didn't have the slightest idea how to start. Maybe they could tell him down at the fire station. The firemen seemed to know almost everything.

Down the street he could see the Pest waiting for him. She had cut through the alley to catch him at the end of his route. Now she was leaning against the high iron fence that ran all around the old Huntley place. Alvin wanted to show off in front of Daphne, even if she was such a tagalong. He loaded the last paper into the tube and pulled back on the special cocking lever. The last house on his route was just beyond the old Huntley place, and he planned to sling the paper within inches of the front door.

But it didn't work out that way. Just as he pedaled past the Pest, the front wheel of the bike hit a crack in the pavement, and his hand jerked down on the special release trigger. The paper whistled out of the Slinger. It sailed right over the Pest's head, across the iron fence and beyond the thick bushes that covered the front of the house. A moment later Alvin heard the tinkle of broken glass.

"Gosh!" said Shoie as he ran up. "What happened?"

"What happened?" repeated the Pest. "I know what happened. Alvin broke a window."

"Doggone crack in the street," mumbled Alvin.

"Yikes, Alvin, what are we going to do about the broken window?" asked Shoie.

"Yes, Alvin, what are we going to do about the broken window?" repeated the Pest.

"Right now I'm not worrying about that broken window," said Alvin. "I'll have plenty of time to worry about it later this morning. Right now I'm worrying about the paper. It was the last one, and I have to have it for Mrs. Perkins. You know how mad she gets when she doesn't get her paper."

"What can you do about it, old bean?" asked Shoie.

Alvin thought for a minute. "I think," he said, "I think I'll go in there after it."

"Oh, Alvin!" gasped Daphne.

The old Huntley place was known as the haunted house of Riverton. Nobody really *believed* it was haunted, because old Mrs. Huntley still lived there, but it certainly looked like a haunted house. In fact, with a high tower on each of the four corners, it looked like a haunted castle that had outlived all the ancient kings and now stood there alone — shabby and neglected. Across the front of the house was a long wooden porch. The wide front steps leaned at a crazy angle, and there were gaping holes where the boards had caved in. Everywhere, the paint was peeling, hanging down here and there in long ribbons that looked like dirty icicles even in the summer.

Around the house ran a high iron fence with spikes

on top. Inside the fence, overgrown bushes and trees almost hid the house from view, giving it a particularly spooky appearance. All the kids said that if you stood at midnight in a certain spot, just outside the fence, and looked up at one of the towers, you'd see a candle moving behind one of the tiny windows. They said this was the ghost of Mr. Huntley, but Alvin didn't believe it. He thought it was probably Mrs. Huntley prowling around the big house at night.

Mrs. Huntley was a very odd old lady to be sure. She believed strange things. For example, she believed that Mr. Huntley, who had been dead twenty years or more, had returned to earth as a bird. In fact, she thought Mr. Huntley was nesting in one of the trees near the house.

Alvin could remember once, two or three years ago, he had been playing near the house and had heard her talking to the birds as she fed them. She had seen him peeking through the bushes and had invited him into the weed-filled yard. There she had shown him how to feed the birds right out of his hand. Alvin was entranced. She was a very kind old lady, he thought, and nothing like a real witch. He had liked her very much. Before he left, she made him promise to feed the birds every day after she died.

Later, when Alvin had told his folks about his visit, they had asked him not to go into the yard again. She was so odd, they said, that he had better leave her to herself. Apparently she liked to be alone. She had no living relatives except a nephew named Herbert who lived in Chicago. Herbert came to see her once a year, a young man with a sly pinched-up face and long black hair. Once when he was in town he had had an argument with the police. Alvin's dad said he was a nasty sort who probably came to see Mrs. Huntley so he could be sure of inheriting her money some day.

Everyone said Mrs. Huntley had lots of money which she kept in a plain paper sack hidden somewhere in the shabby house. She certainly didn't spend much. The people of Riverton seldom saw her on the street, and she wouldn't let anyone on the property to repair the old house or clean it up. She didn't even have electricity. In the middle of the weed patch out behind the house she had a big garden. She refused to eat meat, so people said. Everyone figured that her garden provided all her vegetables as well as the seeds for Mr. Huntley and the rest of the birds.

"Yep," said Alvin to Shoie and the Pest, "I'm going in and get that paper."

"Aren't you scared?" asked the Pest.

"No," said Alvin. "Are you, Shoie?"

"No," said Shoie.

But both of them were a little scared.

Alvin led the way. He had trouble climbing to the top of the high fence, and he tore his pants on one of the big iron spikes. Shoie, the Mighty Athlete, didn't have nearly as much trouble. He just flipped himself up and landed with his feet on the top rail.

"Come on, Pest," said Alvin, reaching down. "Grab hold, and I'll haul you up."

"I'm already in," she answered.

And sure enough, there she was inside the fence. She was small enough to slip between the bars.

The boys dropped to the ground beside her. The grass and weeds came almost to Alvin's waist.

"Lead on, Great Inventor," said Shoie.

"No, the honor should be yours, oh Mighty Athlete," replied Alvin.

But the Pest already was pushing aside the bushes and walking toward the house.

In front of the porch they paused for a moment. Nobody wanted to walk up the old, crazily tilted wooden steps.

Finally, Alvin said, "Come on, I'm going to knock on the door and ask Mrs. Huntley for that paper." He started up the steps.

The Pest promptly caught her foot between two boards. The boys pulled her out, tearing her sock in the process. Then they climbed onto the sagging porch.

"There's the broken window," said Shoie in a whisper. It seemed the most natural thing in the world to whisper.

"Yeah," said Alvin. He tiptoed over to the big window. It was made of little panes of glass, all of them so dusty he could scarcely see into the house.

"Look," said Shoie, beside him. "The mice are eating all the upholstery off the furniture."

"The mice are eating all the upholstery," echoed the Pest in a scared whisper.

Alvin spotted the paper inside the window. He reached through the jagged hole, then drew back his arm.

"Can't reach it," he said.

"Let's get out of here," said Daphne.

Alvin thought for a minute. Finally, he announced, "I'm going to knock on the door. Maybe old Mrs. Huntley will remember me and give me the paper if I promise to fix her window."

The porch floor boards squeaked under his feet. The others followed him to the front door. Alvin paused a minute, then knocked cautiously. There was no answer. He knocked again, rapping his knuckles hard against the weather-beaten wood.

And as he knocked the door swung open with a groan.

"Gosh," said Shoie in a voice so low the others could scarcely hear it.

Alvin glanced back over his shoulder to make sure the others were following. Turning quickly, he walked over to the paper lying on the floor beneath the broken window. Just as he picked it up he jumped as though he had been stung by a hornet.

"Yikes! Look!"

There, on the dusty floor, were two sandwich wrappers from Haggerty's Hamburger Palace. One of them still held part of a sandwich. And nearby were two paper cups, still partially filled with coffee.

"Somebody's been here," whispered Shoie. "Somebody besides old Mrs. Huntley."

"Look at all the footprints in the dust," said Alvin. "Men's footprints."

"Footprints," gasped the Pest.

"Yeah," said Shoie, looking at Alvin. Then, slowly and softly, "Where's Mrs. Huntley? And where are the men who made the footprints? Are they here right now?"

"*Right now!*" shrieked the Pest so loud that both boys jumped. "I'm getting out of here!"

The boys didn't catch up with her until she was almost to the fence. The Mighty Athlete cleared the bars with one bound, but Alvin got snagged on top.

Already Daphne was through the bars and halfway home, her football clutched under her arm.

Chapter 3

THE ELECTRIC PERISCOPE

ALVIN made a point of leaving home right after lunch, before Shoie had time to come over. He was on his way to the firehouse to ask the firemen about a patent on the Paper Slinger, and he didn't want Shoie to find out that he didn't know a thing about it.

There was another thought in the back of his mind as he walked down the street toward the firehouse. Who had been prowling around the old Huntley place? And why?

He'd caught up with his sister, just before she ran into the house, and made her promise not to tell about going into the old Huntley place. If she told, she'd be in trouble, too, for Mom and Dad had warned them not to go inside the iron fence. She finally promised, but Alvin noticed that she'd hung around Mom most of the morning as though she had something on her mind. If she tells, it will just serve her right, thought Alvin.

He walked through the big open door of the fire station. Because his father was a sergeant on the police force, everybody around the police station and the firehouse knew Alvin. He ambled toward the back room, patting the big red fire engine on the fender as he walked by.

"Hi, Mr. McReynolds," he said to the Chief, who was playing cards with some of the other firemen.

19

"Well, hello there, Alvin," said the Chief. "What brings out the great inventor on a day like this?" Alvin's father always told everyone at the police and fire stations about Alvin's inventions.

"Not much," said Alvin, trying to look as though he'd just happened to stop in. He plopped down on a chair and watched them play cards for a few minutes.

Finally he said, "Mr. McReynolds, I know another kid that likes to invent things, too. He made a pretty good invention yesterday and he asked me how to get a patent on it. I told him a lot of stuff about getting a patent, but I thought you might know something I forgot to tell him."

The Chief's eyes twinkled. "So he wants to get a patent, does he? I don't suppose he'd want to tell what his invention is?"

"No. Not yet. Not until he gets a patent. Somebody might steal his invention."

"He must be a pretty smart lad." The Chief looked around the table. "Any of you men know anything about getting a patent."

"A little," said Mr. Sweeney, one of the firemen. "A friend of mine invented a gadget for a car a few years ago. He told me about all the rigamarole he went through to get a patent. He wrote the Patent Office and they sent him some papers to fill out. Later he found out that he had to hire a lawyer to get a patent for him. He finally got it, though, but it cost him quite a lot of money."

Alvin immediately thought of the $2.26 he earned on his paper route each week. "How much?" he asked.

"Seems to me it was close to five hundred dollars."

"Five hundred dollars!" exclaimed Alvin, jumping out of his chair.

"Yep. Just about. He made a few thousand dollars on the invention, though, after it was patented."

Alvin stood there a minute, still dazed by the amount of money he'd need. "Oh," he said. "Five hundred dollars." He started walking toward the door. With his hand on the knob he paused and said, "Thanks. Thanks a lot. I'll tell the other kid. See you later."

"So long, Alvin," said the Chief.

"Good-by," said Mr. Sweeney. "I hope you get your patent, Alvin." He picked up his cards from the table.

Shoie was waiting on the front steps. "Where've you been?" he asked.

"Oh, just downtown."

"I've been thinking about your Paper Slinger," Shoie said. "Maybe we could use it to throw snowballs at some of those guys over on Hickory Street next winter."

"Maybe."

"When are you going to get your patent?"

"Don't know. Soon." Five hundred dollars! Where could he earn that much money?

"That Slinger sure does work fine," said Shoie with admiration. He picked up a rake that was leaning against the house, held it straight up in the air, and balanced it on one finger. "It sure did sling that paper through the window of the old Huntley place."

"Yeah," said Alvin. "I wonder where Mrs. Huntley is, and who else has been in that old house?"

"Maybe some relatives," said Shoie, putting the handle of the rake on his chin. He removed his hands and went staggering across the lawn, balancing the rake.

"Nope. She has only one relative, a nephew who lives in Chicago. There was something funny there, Shoie. Just as I ran out of the room I noticed a flashlight on one of the tables."

"Honest?" asked Shoie, catching the rake.

"Yeah. Let's analyze this problem like an inventor would. Those hamburger wrappers weren't Mrs. Huntley's because everybody says she doesn't eat meat. And that flashlight isn't hers, either. She'd have to buy batteries for it once in awhile, and no one ever sees her downtown. So it must be someone else's flashlight. Shoie, old bean, that flashlight is there for one of two reasons. Either somebody forgot it, or somebody has been around there at night *and is still there or intends to come back again.*"

"Gosh!" said Shoie, trying to balance the rake on his ear this time. "What do you suppose he's doing around that old house?"

"I don't know. But there's probably more than one of them, whoever they are."

"How do you know?" Shoie gave a flip of his hand. The rake flew into the air and he caught it in one hand. He sat down beside Alvin.

"There were two coffee cups."

Shoie looked at him in admiration. "You sure are good at thinking."

"There's something funny going on," repeated Alvin. "If there was no one there, where was Mrs. Huntley?

And if she and a couple of men were there, why didn't they answer the door?"

"Why?" asked Shoie.

"Because they're doing something they shouldn't."

"You're right. I'll bet they're crooks."

Alvin said, "I'm going to find out."

"You are? How?"

"I'm going to take a look after dark tonight."

Shoie gulped. "Honest?"

"Are you coming along?"

"Well," said Shoie. "Well sure, I guess so."

Just then Alvin's mother came to the front door. "Alvin," she asked, "do you know where the broom is?"

"In the front closet," he replied. Suddenly he had a sinking feeling as he heard her rustling through the closet.

She shrieked. "Alvin! What have you done to this broom?"

"I guess I sawed off the handle."

"What in the world for?"

"An invention."

"Alvin," she said. "Alvin, you can't go on this way. Why, the idea of sawing up a perfectly good broom! Young man, I'll speak to your father about this. Furthermore, you'll pay for a new one."

"Yes, Mom," he said.

"Now you just go up to your room and stay there until I say you can come down."

"Yes, Mom." He saw her turn away from the door and walk toward the back of the house. "Come on, Shoie. You come up with me."

As usual, when Alvin got to his room he was thinking so hard about something else that he forgot to turn off the Foolproof Burglar Alarm. The instant he opened the door a bell began to clang, all the lights in the room flashed on and off, and a boxing glove on the end of a long wooden arm came whistling across the doorway. Alvin ducked just in time, but the glove caught Shoie squarely on the ear.

"Doggone it!" yelled Shoie, rubbing the side of his head. "Can't you ever remember to turn that blame thing off before you open the door?"

"Sorry, old man," said Alvin. He closed the door. The bell stopped clanging and the lights went off. Carefully, he cocked the spring that held the glove.

"Come on, Shoie," he said, sitting down on the edge of his bed. "We have work to do."

"What work?" Shoie was still holding his ear.

"We're going to invent an Electric Periscope."

"A what?"

"An Electric Periscope."

"What for?"

"So we can spy on them tonight. Naturally."

"Oh."

Alvin walked over to the table that served as his inventing bench. He searched through several cigar boxes that were jammed with everything from a pair of his mother's eyebrow tweezers to an old hornet's nest. At last he found a little pocket mirror. But one was all he could find.

"I need two of these," he explained. "Come here." He walked over to the doorway and pointed to a push-button. "Hold down on that until I come back. It disconnects the Burglar Alarm."

Alvin sneaked out of the room on tiptoe. He didn't want his mother to hear him. The Pest was standing at the top of the stairs.

"Ssssh," said Alvin, then made a motion with his hand as though he was going to grab her hair. He tiptoed into his mother's room and pulled out a drawer. Inside were a couple of old purses. He hunted through them until he found another little mirror, then tiptoed back to his room and closed the door. Daphne had slipped inside and was standing by his inventing bench.

"What you doing, Alvin?" she asked.

It was Shoie who replied. "He's inventing an Electric

Periscope so we can spy on those ghosts in the old Huntley place."

"Oh," said Daphne.

Alvin measured the mirrors, then cut a long piece of cardboard from the box in which his mother kept his best shirts. The shirts he rolled into a ball and placed on the top shelf of his closet. He rummaged through the cigar boxes until he found a roll of electrician's tape. He folded the piece of cardboard to form a long, square tube, and fastened it with the tape. Then he cut slots, slantwise, in each end of the tube and slipped the mirrors into the slots. In front of each mirror he cut a little window. From the shelf over his bed he took down his small flashlight and taped it to one end of the tube.

For a moment he looked at the invention admiringly. "Not bad," he said. "Not bad for a hurry-up job."

"How does it work?" asked Shoie.

"Pull down the window shade and I'll show you."

When the room was dark, Alvin crawled behind the bed. "Can you see me?" he called.

"Not when you're behind the bed in this dim light."

Alvin stuck one end of the tube over the bed, the end with the flashlight. He turned on the light. "Wow!" he exclaimed. "Perfect."

"Let me see," said Shoie.

The boys traded places. Shoie, lying on the floor, looked into the window in one end of the tube. He could see Alvin, plain as day, standing on the other side of the room. "Gee," he said, "that's a pretty good invention. How does it work?"

"There's nothing to it, really," said Alvin, though he was pleased as punch. "That mirror on top sees a picture of me. It sends it on to the bottom mirror, where you can see it."

"But Alvin," said the Pest, "if you're going to spy on somebody, won't they see the light from your flashlight?"

Alvin shook his head as though he were disgusted. Actually, he hadn't even thought of that problem. Finally he said, "Criminently! Do you think I'm that dumb? Of course they'll have their own lights. That light on the Electric Periscope is only for emergency use.

"Oh," said the Pest.

"I wonder who they are," said Shoie, unconsciously lowering his voice.

"We'll know tonight," said Alvin. "I'll set my Silent Waker Upper for eleven-thirty and sneak over to your place. Leave your window wide open and I'll toss a rock through it to wake you up."

"For gosh sakes, make it a small one," said Shoie. "You've already done enough damage to me with that darn Burglar Alarm."

"Can I look through the Periscope now?" asked Daphne.

"No. You keep your hands off."

"I'll tell Mama what you're going to do tonight."

"You hadn't better," threatened Alvin. "Here, take a look."

The Pest looked up at her big brother. She thought he was a genius.

Chapter 4

A NARROW ESCAPE

THE string jerked Alvin awake. For a moment he wondered if the Silent Waker Upper had gone haywire. It seemed as though he hadn't been in bed very long. Suddenly he remembered. The old Huntley place! He reached down in the darkness, turned off the alarm, and slipped the string off his toe.

Dressing quietly in the dark, he put on sneakers so he wouldn't make much noise during the big adventure. If his folks knew what he was planning, he'd be scalped.

Alvin tied a string to the Electric Periscope, then looped it around his neck so both hands would be free. He eased a chair over to the closet, climbed up, and took from the top shelf his Portable Fire Escape. It was a long rope that ran over a bunch of pulleys. The rope was snarled into a big ball, and he had trouble untangling it in the dark. Some fire escape, he thought. What if the house were on fire right now? Finally, he managed to untangle it. He tied one end of the rope to the leg of his bed and threw the other end out the open window.

Hitching up his belt, he crawled out the window and started letting himself down the side of the house. Halfway down he bumped the house. He hung there motionless for a minute, but there wasn't a peep from inside. At last he let himself down to the end of the rope, kicked his feet wildly, and let loose. His foot

struck something soft just before he hit the ground.

"Ouch!" said a voice. "Can't you watch where you're going, Alvin?" It was the Pest, of course, standing there in her nightgown.

Alvin's nerves were jumpy. At first he was startled, then angry. "Criminently, can't I do anything without you spying on me? You go right back to bed. And do it quietly so the folks won't hear you."

"I'm going with you, Alvin."

"No you're not. You're going back to bed!"

"If you don't take me along I'll holler just as loud as I can. Like this." The Pest opened her mouth as if she were going to scream.

"Ssssh!" said Alvin. "Do you want the folks to hear you?"

"Yes."

Alvin thought for a minute. There didn't seem to be any way out of it. "All right, but remember, this is your own idea to tag along. Don't blame me if anything happens. And you've got to promise you won't get in our way."

"Won't get in your way," she repeated.

Alvin walked down the moonlit street with his sister at his heels. When he got to Shoie's house, he dodged from tree to tree, imitating the guys on television. He reached the gravel driveway and crept along the side of the house until he was just beneath Shoie's second-floor window. He picked up a stone and pitched it up through the window. It made a terrible clatter inside, but nothing happened.

Alvin tossed a bigger stone toward the window. In

the darkness, he couldn't see where it went and was just stooping over for another when it came down and hit him on the ear.

"Ouch!" he said, then clapped his hand over his mouth. He rubbed his ear for a minute, then tossed another stone. There was a crash of broken glass inside the house. Lights began winking on all over the second floor.

Alvin pushed his sister behind some bushes and crouched beside her. He heard a door open in the room above his head.

"Wilfred!" said Shoie's mother, who always called him Wilfred. "Wilfred, are you all right?"

"Yeah, I'm okay, Mom."

"For heaven's sake, what happened to your mirror?"

There was a long pause. Then Shoie's voice said, "I guess I was dreaming, Mom. I guess I was dreaming about playing baseball, and maybe I threw a wild pitch."

"How many times have I told you not to take that ball and glove to bed with you?"

"I won't do it again, Mom."

"Good heavens, what a mess. Well, leave it until morning. But don't walk around in here without your shoes, Wilfred. You'll cut your feet on all that broken glass."

"I won't, Mom."

One by one the lights in the house winked out. Shoie's head popped through the window. "I'll be down in a minute," he whispered.

Soon Shoie appeared at the window. He came out backwards, climbing down until he was hanging onto

the window sill, his legs dangling in space. Then he
started swinging his body back and forth.

Just as Alvin thought Shoie couldn't hang on another
second, the swinging feet reached far out and touched
the roof of the back porch. Shoie scrambled onto the
roof, crawled to the corner of the house, and shinnied
down the downspout, landing on his feet beside them.

"Well done, oh Mighty Athlete," said Alvin. "But
how will you get back up?"

"Got the front door key in my pocket," whispered
Shoie. "I just did that for show. Boy, you should see
what you did to my mirror."

"Sorry, old bean."

"You're forgiven, old man."

"Quite so, old bean."

"Let's get on with our plans, old man."

"Quite so, beans," said the Pest.

"Sssssh!" said Alvin.

He led the way down to the corner, then up the street
toward the old Huntley place.

By the time they left the last street light and were
moving through the darkness, Alvin wasn't so sure he
wanted to go through with his plan. To tell the truth,
he was downright scared, but he couldn't let the others
know it. He had done too much talking to back out now.

"Alvin, let's go back," said Daphne.

The sudden sound of her voice made Alvin jump
sideways, but he quickly recovered and kept right on
jumping back and forth down the sidewalk, as though
that were part of his plan.

At the iron fence Alvin paused for a moment, then

climbed to the top. He took a deep breath and leaped into the black shrubbery below. A moment later Shoie was standing beside him. This time, Alvin noticed, the Pest waited until they were inside before she slipped through the bars. She pressed up against Alvin, shivering in her thin nightgown. Alvin felt a little shivery, too.

"We'll keep together," he announced in a whisper. That suited the others fine.

They crept through the shrubbery and weeds until they could see the old house. Suddenly they all stopped.

"Look!" said Shoie.

"EEEEEEEeeeeee" Daphne started to scream, and Alvin clamped his hand over her mouth.

Up in one of the towers a dim light was moving, casting spooky shadows across the windowpanes.

For a long time they squatted there in the weeds,

watching. The shadows moved back and forth across the window. At last the light winked out.

"Whew," sighed Shoie.

"Looked like ghosts," said Alvin.

"*Ghosts!*" repeated Daphne in a whispered shriek. "I'm going home to Mommy!" Alvin grabbed her arm and held her until she stopped shaking.

"Maybe we all ought to go home," suggested Shoie.

Alvin felt the same way, but he didn't want to show it. Finally the magnificent brain began analyzing the situation.

"Can't be ghosts," he said. "In the first place, there isn't such a thing as a ghost, and in the second place, ghosts wouldn't be drinking coffee and eating hamburgers."

"That's right," whispered Shoie.

"So it must be people. And if it's people, we're going to find out what they're doing. We're going through with our plan."

Alvin acted a lot braver than he felt as he sneaked through the weeds toward the house. He kept glancing back over his shoulder to make sure the others were following. He didn't know what was in front of him, but he wanted something familiar behind his back.

At the rickety steps to the porch they stopped and glanced up at the gloomy house. In the moonlight it looked more than ever like a deserted castle.

"What are you going to do, Alvin?" asked Shoie.

Alvin didn't know exactly what he was going to do, so he crouched there as though he were deciding which of several plans to use.

A light suddenly moved into the big room almost directly in front of them, the room with the broken window.

The three figures at the bottom of the steps could have been statues as they watched the light shining eerily on the dusty window. They could hear muffled voices, but couldn't make out any of the words.

For long minutes they crouched there, watching the light move back and forth and listening to the voices. Finally, Alvin got a cramp in his big toe and stood up.

"I'm going to take a look," he whispered, reaching around his back for his Electric Periscope. In the darkness he tried to untie the string, but the knot wouldn't come unsnarled. And the more he worked with the knot, the higher it slipped around his neck, until it started to bite into his skin. He was beginning to gasp when Shoie saw that he was in trouble. Shoe's two strong hands broke the string.

"Argle," said Alvin, trying to get his voice back. He took a deep breath and rubbed his neck. "Thanks for saving my life."

"Let's go home, beans!" whispered the Pest.

"Quiet," said Alvin. He crawled up the steps, then squirmed across the porch floor on his stomach. He could hear the rustle of Shoie and the Pest behind him.

Alvin was afraid to look directly into the window. He figured whoever was inside would spot his white face through the pane. But if he could only get the Electric Periscope into position, it wouldn't be seen nearly so easily.

Lying beneath the window, Alvin took a deep breath and eased the top of the Periscope above the window sill. He peered into the hole at the bottom.

For a minute Alvin couldn't make out a thing. Slowly, he turned the Periscope. The chewed-up sofa, the battered old piano appeared. He turned the Periscope farther. There, right in front of his eyes, was the back of a man's head.

Alvin turned the Periscope still more. This time he was almost blinded by the beam of a large flashlight lying on the table. And beside the table he could see another man, a short man with a thin face and long hair. The man's lips were moving, and Alvin could hear his voice but couldn't understand a word that was said. And there was no sign of old Mrs. Huntley.

He shifted the Periscope back to the other man and saw him walk across the room to the sofa. There he did a strange thing. He started ripping the sofa cushions apart. The stuffing seemed to fly all over the room. When the last cushion was in shreds, the man threw the rags to the floor in a gesture of disgust.

At the sound of a voice Alvin swung the Periscope back to the first man. He was walking across the room to the piano. He lifted the piano lid, pointed the flashlight inside, and looked for a long time. Then he slammed down the lid. Both men sat down again, the flashlight on the floor at their feet.

"What's going on?" Shoie whispered in Alvin's ear.

Alvin didn't want to give up the Periscope, but he had to admit that Shoie deserved a look. He handed it over and crouched there, thinking. Of one thing Alvin was certain. The two men were searching for something, and were angry because they couldn't find it. What could it be?

The Pest snuggled up against him and said in his ear, "Let me look, Alvin." Her shrill little voice seemed loud on the moonlit porch.

"No," he hissed. He grabbed the Periscope from Shoie and had another look himself. The men were still seated in their chairs, talking.

"I want to look, Alvin," insisted Daphne.

"No!" He pushed her hand away.

"I'm going to look," she announced. She reached up for the Electric Periscope, grabbed it at the top and began pulling.

To Alvin, it seemed that the world caved in on him in a fraction of a second. A new beam of light suddenly spotlighted the two men inside the house. Instantly, Alvin realized in horror that it was the beam from the Periscope. His sister must have pushed the switch while she was trying to grab it out of his hands.

Alvin couldn't seem to tear his eye away from the Periscope. He saw the thin-faced man leap from his chair and rush toward the window. A moment later the man was so close that all Alvin could see were the buttons on his coat.

Shoie reached the steps first and didn't bother to run down them. He flew through the air and landed in the weeds. Daphne tumbled into the bushes at his heels. Alvin was halfway across the porch when he realized that he had dropped his great invention. He was back

at the window in two steps, grabbed his Periscope, and ran for his life. His foot touched just one step on the way down, and at that instant he heard the door open behind his back.

Alvin ran through the weeds faster than he had ever run in the school relays. His feet barely touched the ground. He expected to hear someone shout at him, but all he heard was the swish of feet running through the weeds at his back.

He saw a white figure moving just ahead of him. As he passed his sister he reached out an arm and snared her around the waist. He half-dragged her toward the street. Now the footsteps were swishing along at his heels.

In the dim moonlight he spotted Shoie atop the fence. He shoved Daphne through the bars, then leaped upward. The Mighty Athlete caught him by the collar, and Alvin felt himself lifted to the top of the fence. Something grabbed one leg of his trousers from below. He jerked his leg free, and both boys dropped to the other side of the fence.

The Pest was already racing down the street toward home, her nightgown flapping around her legs. Alvin and Shoie sensed two faces pressed against the bars, but they didn't even take time for a glance as they chased after Daphne.

A voice called through the darkness, "Come back, kids. We won't hurt you. Come back!"

The boys were too scared even to turn around. At the corner Shoie peeled off and headed for home without a word. Alvin followed the Pest through the door and crept upstairs at her heels. He heard her run into her room on tiptoe, then the creak of her bed.

For once in his life Alvin remembered to push the hidden button outside the door that disconnected the Foolproof Burglar Alarm. Inside the room, he shut the door as quietly as he could, dropped the Electric Periscope on his workbench, ripped off his clothes and hopped into his pajamas.

Only when he was under the covers did Alvin feel safe. And even then a frightening thought crept into his mind. Suppose the two men had chased them down the street and saw which house they went into? Suppose, even now, they were creeping around downstairs trying to find him?

Alvin threw back the covers, leaped across the room and flipped the switch to connect the Foolproof Burglar Alarm once more. He raced over to the window and hauled up the Portable Fire Escape. Then he dived back into bed and pulled the covers over his head.

Chapter 5

THE SUPERSECRET EAVESDROPPER

FOR a moment after the Silent Waker Upper jerked at his toe, Alvin had the feeling that he'd dreamed the whole adventure — that it was just another nightmare. Then he looked over at the Electric Periscope on the workbench and realized that it had really happened.

Alvin dressed slowly. This morning, for some reason, he didn't want to go out on his paper route. Particularly, he didn't want to ride down the street in front of the old Huntley place.

When he slipped into the Pest's room, all he could see was a little ball under the covers. Her room was a sight to behold. Daphne's mother had fixed up the room with all the frills that should be dear to a girl's heart. At the windows were Priscilla curtains, and a dust ruffle ran around the bottom of the bed. In one corner was a dressing table with a matching ruffle around it. Ballerinas danced daintily across the wallpaper. But Daphne was a tomboy. Her worn baseball glove and half-inflated football rested on the dressing table, jet airplanes hung from the ceiling by invisible threads, and she had covered most of the ballerinas with baseball trading cards. No question about it, Daphne was a tomboy.

Alvin turned back the blanket and saw her lying there sleeping peacefully. Gently, he put his hand over her mouth. Her eyes opened slowly and she blinked a couple

of times. Suddenly, she was staring up at him, her mouth wide open as she remembered what had happened.

"Sorry to wake you up," he said in a low voice, "but I wanted to warn you not to tell Mom or Dad about what happened last night. If you do, they'll probably make us stay in for weeks, and you'll have to do the dishes every meal."

"I think they should know," said the Pest.

He tried to think of something that would keep her from talking. "If you tell," he said, "if you tell, I — I — well, I won't ever let you look at any of my inventions again."

He could see her working this threat over in her mind. Always, she had been fascinated by his inventions.

Finally she said, "If I don't tell, will you promise to show me every invention you ever make?"

He nodded his head. "Every single one."

"Even if you live to be a hundred?"

"Even if I live to be a hundred," he promised.

"Cross your heart?"

He crossed his heart.

"Well, okay. But if you don't keep your promise, I'm going to tell right away."

Alvin was a little slower than usual on his paper route that morning. In the first place, Shoie didn't show up to help him. And somehow he didn't have any desire to use his Paper Slinger.

When he finally forced himself to ride down the street in front of the old Huntley place, he pedaled as fast as he could. He had the feeling someone might be watching him. Once he glanced toward the bushes, but didn't see anything.

Later that morning Alvin went to work on an invention that had been in the back of his mind for quite some time. It was an Automatic Lawn Mower Guider. Even though he was allowed to use Dad's power mower, he still hated to mow the lawn.

He was about to give his new invention a test when Shoie came walking down the street.

"Hi, old bean," said Shoie. "What are you doing?"

"Working on my Automatic Lawn Mower Guider," said Alvin.

Neither of them asked the question that had worried both of them all morning. Where was old Mrs. Huntley? She kept popping up in Alvin's thoughts, but their adventure of the night before had been so scary he didn't want to say anything about her. He was certain his parents would punish him if they found out he had been sneaking around the old house at night. In the back of his mind, Alvin knew that sooner or later he'd have to face up to the problem of old Mrs. Huntley. But right now he couldn't force himself to say anything about her.

He went right on working on his invention. He dug a hole in the middle of the front lawn, put an old piece of a fence post in it, then stomped back the dirt so the fence post stuck a couple of feet out of the lawn. He went to the garage, wheeled out the power mower, and put it way out on the edge of the lawn. Unfastening his mother's clothesline from the clothes poles, he tied one end of the rope to the lawn mower, the other to the post.

By this time Shoie was getting interested. "How does it work, Alvin?"

"Well, with this good old invention I can sit on the porch and watch the power mower do all the work. I can even go in the house, mix up a glass of lemonade, come back out, and the mower will have been working all that time.

"Here's how it will work. I'll start up the mower, put it in gear, and it will go forward by itself. This rope will hold it so it won't mow straight, but in a big circle around the post. As it goes around the post, the rope will wind up, so the circle will get smaller and smaller. Pretty soon the mower will be right in against the post and the whole lawn will be mowed, except for a little trimming around the edges."

"Gosh!" said Shoie. "You sure do have wild ideas."

Alvin jerked the starter rope a couple of times before he remembered that he had taken an important spring off the mower to use on his Automatic Shoe Shiner. He went inside, returned with the spring, and put it back on the mower. This time the mower started with one jerk.

He checked the long rope and the post, then put the mower in gear. It started across the lawn, pulling against the rope. But instead of moving in a straight line, it moved in a huge circle right around the post.

Alvin ran over and sat down on the front steps with Shoie. They both watched in admiration as the mower circled the post, the grass clippings flying out behind.

"Yippee!" said Shoie, leaping up and chasing the

mower. For the first time that day, he seemed like the old Shoie. He ran back over to Alvin and pounded him on the back. "Yippee! The Great Inventor has done it again."

Just then — disaster!

Both boys were watching as the mower hit a bump in the lawn, gave a bounce, and jerked the post right out of the ground. Then, trailing the rope and fence post, it rolled across the lawn toward the flower bed.

Alvin and Shoie couldn't move. They watched in horror as the mower plowed right through the flowers. Snapdragons and daisies flew in every direction. At the last minute it veered toward a new bed of pansies, clipped them neatly to the ground, hit the fence, coughed twice and stopped.

At that moment Alvin's mother stuck her head out the door.

Alvin didn't particularly mind being sent to his room because it gave him a chance to work on his inventions, but he always complained bitterly so his mother wouldn't catch on. Today, he worked on his Super Robot. By late afternoon he had succeeded in making the Robot's eyes flash on and off, and fixed it so the Robot would reach one arm jerkily across and scratch the opposite ear.

The Robot didn't seem nearly as much fun as he'd thought it would, though, because no matter how hard he worked on it, he kept thinking about Mrs. Huntley. He remembered the time, long ago, when she had made him promise to feed all the birds around her house if anything ever happened to her. He could see her now, a kindly smile on her wrinkled face as the birds flocked around her. Well, had something happened to her? And wasn't it up to him to find out?

Suddenly the thought struck him. Perhaps he could find out what had happened to Mrs. Huntley without his folks knowing anything about it. Then, if she was all right, his folks need never know that he had disobeyed them by going back to the old house. And if something *had* happened to her . . . Well, he'd face that problem when he came to it.

At last, when his mother relented and let him go outdoors, a plan had taken shape in his mind. He headed for the garage, climbed up the rose trellis, and clambered onto the roof. He focused the Long Distance Signal Mirror so it would catch the sun's rays and reflect them up the street into Shoie's bedroom window. He waggled his hand over the mirror, spelling the letters in Morse code:

```
_ ._. _ _ _ _ .   ._    _ _ _ _. _._.
C   O   M  E   A T   O   N   C   E
_.. . ..._ . ._.. _ _ _ .__. .. _ _.   _. . .__
D  E  V  E  L  O   P   I N G    N E  W
.. _. ..._ . _. _ .. _ _ _ _.
I  N  V  E  N T I  O  N
```

By the time he'd shinnied back down to the ground Shoie was racing up the street.

"Hi, old bean," said Shoie, a little out of breath. "So she finally let you out of prison. What's up?"

"Need your help, old man," replied Alvin. "Got to work fast. We're going to need this invention tonight, so don't waste any time. No questions. First thing I want you to do is unscrew the hose off the faucet at the back of the house and drag both ends of it around here. I'll be back in a minute."

"What —" began Shoie.

"No questions. Just do as I say."

Shoie raced for the back of the house and Alvin ran for the front door. In the coat closet he tossed out sweaters, jackets, coats, and hats until he found what he wanted — an old winter cap he'd worn a couple of years before. It was made like an aviator's helmet, with ear flaps that were held tight around his face by a strap under his chin.

Alvin raced out to the garage and found the funnel that he used to pour gasoline into the lawn mower. For a moment he stood there shuddering at the thought of the mower. He squared his shoulders and went back out the garage door. Shoie was standing there with the two ends of the hose in his hands.

Alvin handed Shoie the funnel. "Push the funnel into one end of the hose," he said.

While Shoie was doing that, Alvin found a bit of tape in his pocket. "Wind that around the funnel and the hose, so the funnel won't come out," he instructed.

Alvin started working on the old winter hat. He put it on his head, checking it for size, and found that it was considerably too small. He couldn't pull it down as far as it should be, so there was some extra space above the top of his head.

Shoie looked at him and grinned. "Room for your point, old bean," he said.

Alvin didn't think it was very funny. With his finger, he held the place where his ear came under one of the flaps, then took off the hat. He marked the place with a pencil. Opening his knife, he carefully cut a little X at that point.

He held out his hand, palm up, toward Shoie. Shoie looked at him with a puzzled expression, then handed him the end of the hose with the funnel.

Alvin shook his head. "The other end, stupid," he said. "Watch what you're doing or I'll fire you."

Shoie shrugged and handed him the other end of the hose. Alvin put the cut in the hat over it, and pushed down. There was a little rip as he forced the hat over the end of the hose. Then he turned the helmet inside out, puckered up the cloth around the end of the hose and tied the helmet in place with a piece of string.

When he had finished, the hat was tightly bound to

the end of the hose. The hose stuck inside the hat at a point where it would touch his ear.

"There!" said Alvin, admiring his work. "A fast job, but a good one. I'll bet it works, too."

"What is it?" asked Shoie.

"A Supersecret Eavesdropper," replied Alvin patiently, as though anyone should know what it was.

"What's an Eavesdropper?"

"Why, anybody knows what an Eavesdropper is. You use it to listen to other people talk, without letting them know you're listening."

"Oh," said Shoie. "How does it work?"

"I'll show you. Take the funnel end of the hose — that's the microphone — around to the other side of the house."

Shoie disappeared around the corner, dragging the hose with him.

Alvin waited until he felt a jerk on the hose. He gave it a jerk to stop Shoie, then put on the hat. He could feel the end of the hose right against his ear. For three or four minutes he waited, but couldn't hear a thing. Maybe the Supersecret Eavesdropper was a failure. . . .

He shouted, "Well, say something!"

On the other end of the hose, Shoie heard the shout. He put his lips down to the funnel and shouted as loud as he could, "I didn't know you wanted me to talk to you." He waited a couple of minutes, but didn't hear anything from Alvin. Finally he dropped the funnel and ran around the house. Alvin was stumbling around in circles, holding his ear.

"What's the matter?" asked Shoie.

Alvin groaned. "I didn't tell you to shout. I just told you to say something. Ohhhhh, my ear."

Alvin sat down and waggled his head back and forth for two or three minutes. Finally he said, "Okay, let's try it again. Only this time, just whisper into the funnel."

Shoie ran back around the house and picked up the funnel. He didn't know exactly what to whisper. Finally, in a very low voice, he said, "My dad can beat up your dad any day of the week, blindfolded, with one hand tied behind his back and a bad case of measles."

He heard Alvin shout back, "Don't let my dad hear you say that, old bean."

Shoie ran around the house, turned a cartwheel, landed on Alvin's toe and pounded him on the back. "Gosh, it works. It works!"

Alvin hopped around, trying to hold his toe and rub his back at the same time. "Careful, oh Mighty Athlete," he said. "You don't know your own strength."

"Let me try it, old bean."

This time Shoie put on the hat and listened while Alvin whispered. Alvin's voice came through loud and clear, "No wonder you scratch so much. You're covered with fleas."

They took turns insulting each other for awhile. Finally, they sat down together behind the house to admire the Supersecret Eavesdropper.

"What's the hat for, Alvin?" asked Shoie. "Couldn't you just hold the end of the hose against your ear and hear just as well?"

The great inventor spoke to Shoie in the same tone he frequently used on the Pest. "That'd be some invention, wouldn't it. Every time you wanted to listen you'd have to hold a hose against your ear. Some invention!" He shook his head. "Besides, we'll need both hands free when we use this Supersecret Eavesdropper tonight."

"What do you mean?" asked Shoie. He knew what Alvin meant, but he didn't want to put it into words.

"You know what I mean. We're going back to the old Huntley place and listen to those two men. We're going to find out what happened to Mrs. Huntley."

Shoie shuddered. "Maybe you are. I'm not."

"Don't tell me the Mighty Athlete is scared."

"Of course I'm scared. Aren't you?"

"Well, maybe — just a little," Alvin admitted. "But we've got to find out what they're doing in that old house."

"Why?"

"Just because it's our duty to find out about old Mrs. Huntley. Maybe she's hurt, or — or something."

"Or something," said Shoie, "something else. Maybe she's — maybe she's *dead*."

Alvin was silent.

Finally Shoie said, "But I don't *want* to go back to that spooky old house, Alvin."

"We've *got* to. Now are you coming along, or are you going to chicken out?"

"Cluck-cluck-cluck," said Shoie.

"Oh, come on, Shoie. With this invention —" he motioned toward the Supersecret Eavesdropper "with this invention we'll be perfectly safe. Why, we can lie in the bushes a long way from the house and hear everything they're saying."

"I don't know, Alvin," said Shoie doubtfully.

Alvin had an inspiration. "I'll tell you what, old man. I've got a great invention all worked out in my mind. It's a pair of Kangaroo Shoes with big springs hidden in them. You'll be able to walk down the street in front of everybody, as though you were wearing an ordinary pair of shoes. Then, whenever you want to, you can press a button on your belt and go sailing fifteen, maybe twenty feet in the air. Why, that's as high as a house. Think of it! If you'll come along tonight, I'll give you my Kangaroo Shoes as soon as I invent them."

Shoie was fascinated. Why, with those shoes he could beat the high-jump record easily. "You're sure we'll be safe tonight?" he asked cautiously.

"Absolutely sure. Cross my heart."

"Well, okay then. I'll come along. But just for a little while."

Before Shoie left, Alvin told him to tie a string around his wrist when he went to bed and dangle the other end out the window. That way he wouldn't have to throw any more rocks into Shoie's room.

As Alvin went in to wash up for supper, he saw his sister come around the corner of the house. He groaned. He'd promised to show her every invention, and if she thought he was trying to hide the Supersecret Eavesdropper, she'd go straight to his folks and tell them everything. Well, he supposed he'd have to show it to her.

The Pest, of course, knew exactly how to get anything she wanted from Alvin. And before he knew what had happened, she not only had seen the Supersecret Eavesdropper, but knew all about his plans to find out what had happened to Mrs. Huntley by listening in on the two men that night.

"But you're not tagging along this time," he said as they went into the house.

"Tag along," she echoed.

Chapter 6

UP A TREE

THE three figures sneaked down the deserted street trying to avoid the pools of light beneath the street lights. Alvin, with the Supersecret Eavesdropper coiled over his shoulder, was annoyed with himself. Some magnificent brain! Why, he couldn't even keep his kid sister from knowing everything he did.

He looked down at her in the moonlight and his thoughts softened. She was sort of appealing, all right, trudging along beside him in her jeans. He wished she hadn't come, though. No telling what might happen.

The closer they got to the old Huntley place, the less Alvin wanted to go through with his plan. Seemed like it was darker tonight — and spookier.

They managed to climb the fence without making much noise. In the bushes on the other side they huddled together for a moment, then moved on.

As they crept through the grass, Alvin looked up and saw the big black house silhouetted against the skyline. It was a scary sight — scary enough to make a tickle run down anybody's spine.

"*Whoooooo!*" The sound came from above their heads. Alvin just about jumped out of his skin.

"*Whoooooo!*"

The three children hugged the ground.

"*Whoooooo!*"

Suddenly Alvin knew what it was. "An owl," he whispered to the others. "Only an owl. Probably Mr. Huntley, back to haunt the place — that's whooooooo."

On up toward the house they crept. Finally, Alvin stopped beneath a tree.

"This is our listening post," he whispered. "We'll stretch the hose on up to the house from here." He looked at Shoie. "Are you coming?"

"No thanks. You promised we'd be safe, and this is as close as I'm going to get to that house tonight."

"Scardy!"

"Okay, I'm scared." Shoie stretched out on the ground as though he'd never move.

Alvin handed him the helmet. "You and Pest climb up in the tree where you'll be safe, and there's no chance they'll see you if they come prowling around out here. Hang onto the helmet. I'll take the microphone up to the house alone, as long as you're too scared to help me."

He crept off through the grass, the hose snaking along behind him. Now that he was alone, the closer he got the spookier it seemed. At the bottom of the rickety steps he paused a minute and looked up.

There was a faint light in the window, as though it were shining into the big front room from the back of the house.

Even though the night air was cool, Alvin could feel the sweat trickle down his face. He knelt there a moment, heart pounding. Then he started crawling up the steps.

A board creaked under his knees.

There wasn't a sound from inside the house for two or three minutes. Alvin finally crawled on up until he was lying on the porch. Then, squirming on his stomach, he made his way across the old floorboards until he was just beneath the broken window. Holding the funnel up to the window, he suddenly realized that he had completely forgotten something. How was he going to fasten the funnel in the jagged opening? He lowered the funnel, and took time to hit himself softly on his head.

Then he thought of the loose floorboards. His hands crept across the floor until they found a board that felt particularly loose. Only one nail seemed to be holding it so he pried up the board with his fingers.

Screeeeeeech!

Alvin thought the sound of that rusty nail could be heard clear down at the fire station. Surely the two men would hear it. He held his breath.

Still there was no sound from inside. He forced himself to put the funnel back up against the window so that part of it extended over the hole. He propped it in that position with the floorboard. It was tipsy, but it seemed to hold all right.

As fast as he could, he crawled back to join the others. Shoie was hanging onto a limb with both hands, the helmet over his head. Alvin climbed up into the tree beside him.

"All set," he said. "Heard anything yet?"

"Not a peep," answered Shoie. "Are you sure there's anyone in there?"

"Yep." Alvin held out his hand. Shoie took off the earphone and gave it to him.

For a long time Alvin listened without any luck. After a while he could sense from the wriggling in the

tree that the other two were growing impatient. Perhaps his plan was a failure. The ear flaps were hot around his ears, and he was just reaching up to take off the hat when he thought he heard something.

There it was again. This time he heard it distinctly. A door slamming!

Alvin touched the others on the shoulder, pointed to the earphone and nodded his head.

A voice came through a little muffled, but clear enough to be understood. "I know it's here somewhere. Years ago, she told me it was."

A second voice, much deeper, answered: "Yeah, we both know it's here. But we aren't finding it."

First voice: "Let's sit down and think about this for a minute."

Second voice: "That's all we been doing. Thinking."

First voice: "We've looked in all the obvious places. Let's use our heads. Where would you hide it if you knew somebody was going to be looking for it?"

Second voice: "She's pretty smart. She probably located a hiding place where *nobody* could find it."

First voice: "Maybe."

A long pause.

First voice: "Once she told me it was in a paper sack." Pause. "Now where would she hide a paper sack jammed with thousands of dollars?"

Alvin almost fell out of the tree. Thousands of dollars! *Thousands of dollars!*

Second voice: "We could look through every room in the house again. But we've already been through every room twice. Wish she wasn't so stubborn, and there was some way we could make her tell. I'm about ready to give up."

First voice: "You want to turn your back on all that money?"

A pause. Second voice: "No. But do you have any new ideas?"

First voice: "No. But we sure don't have time to go through the whole house again. I'm surprised those kids haven't been back already with their parents."

Alvin held tighter to the tree.

Second voice: "I have a hunch they won't be back. They'd have shown up before this if they'd squealed. I'll bet we scared 'em so bad they slept with the covers over their heads."

How right he is, thought Alvin.

First voice: "Well, this isn't finding the loot. Let's look over this room once more."

There was a rustle in the earphone.

First voice: "What's that thing over there?"

Second voice: "What thing?"

First voice: "Right there."

Long pause.

Second voice: "Why, uh, why — why, that's just an old — vase."

Alvin thought there was a strange note in his voice, a mighty strange note.

First voice (speaking in a rush) : "We'll search every room of the house again. Yeah, that's what we'll do. We'll start with the basement. This time we'll even look inside the furnace and up the chimney. Then we'll work our way up. We'll look in every room on this floor. We'll take apart the piano. When we've finished here, we'll go upstairs and even search the towers."

Alvin thought it was odd that only one man was talking now. Not a peep from the other one.

First voice, droning on: "We'll even look on the roof. Then, when we're through inside the house, we'll start outside. We'll —"

Too late, Alvin suddenly realized what had happened. They'd spotted the funnel! There was only one man inside the room, and he was talking to himself!

At that instant, a bright beam of light flashed up into the tree from below. They'd been found!

"Got you!" said Second Voice from behind the blinding light. "Followed that hose right to your little nest. Got you this time!"

Daphne whimpered, but was too scared to make much noise.

"Come on out," the man shouted toward the house. "I've caught them in a tree. Come on out, and we'll show them what we do to spying kids."

For a moment Alvin was paralyzed. Then suddenly his brain went into action. He whispered to Shoie, "When I shout, jump right into that flashlight with your feet."

Alvin waited a moment until he heard the front door slam. An instant later he jerked the hose just as hard as he could, and shouted, "Now!"

Shoie dropped down out of the tree, and at that moment Alvin felt a satisfying ripple along the hose. There was a loud thud from the direction of the house. He'd tripped the man on the front steps with the hose.

Another thud came from below, and then the flashlight was spinning off into the grass.

"Yow!" shouted the man beneath him, and Alvin knew that Shoie had dropped out of the tree right onto the man's arm. The Mighty Athlete had come through.

Alvin dropped to the ground. The Pest landed beside him. It was dark under the tree and he could hear the man groaning in the bushes. He and the Pest raced after Shoie, who was heading for the fence.

Alvin could hear stumbling steps behind him, then the pound of running feet. Once more he was atop the fence, with Shoie and the Pest already racing down the street.

Just before Alvin jumped off the fence, he glanced back at the old house. There was a flickering light in the window of one of the towers. Did he imagine it, or was there a head silhouetted against the window?

He jumped off the fence, but he was too late. An arm reached between the bars and grabbed his jacket. No matter how hard Alvin squirmed, he couldn't wriggle loose until he simply slid out of the jacket, leaving it in the man's hand, and ran off down the street.

He had trouble going to sleep that night. His inventive mind had earned a long rest, but an hour passed before it relaxed into a troubled sleep.

Chapter 7

THE ONE-JERK BED MAKER

AFTER breakfast Alvin headed for his room to make his bed. It was a job he didn't like one bit, a job for girls. Long ago, though, he had learned not to argue about it or forget to do it. When he complained that only girls should make beds, his mother made him put on an apron and wipe the dishes. When he forgot to do it, she ordered him to make all the other beds in the house. Consequently, he had learned to make his bed first thing after breakfast.

He was pulling up the sheet and blanket when a sudden thought struck him. A glassy look came across his eyes, and he sat down on the edge of the bed. For five minutes he stared off into space. Suddenly he leaped to his feet, raced downstairs, and returned with two of his mother's spring-action clothespins.

Rummaging through the boxes on his inventing bench, he found a ball of strong cord and two small pulleys. He tied the pulleys to the head of the bed, one on each side of the pillow. He cut two long pieces of cord. One end of each cord he tied to one of the clothespins. The other ends he ran through the pulleys. He brought the cords down under the bed, leaving plenty of slack on the floor, then tied the two cords to the footboard. He squeezed open two clothespins and fastened one to the sheet and blanket on each side of the bed.

Alvin was about to try another great invention. He climbed into bed, pulled up the covers, closed his eyes and tossed about as though he were asleep. A couple of minutes of hard sleep and the bed was a mess, but the sheet and blanket were still tucked in at the foot. Alvin rolled out of bed and walked around to the footboard. He stood there a moment, holding the two cords, almost afraid to try the invention.

He pulled slowly on the cords. The blanket and sheet slid neatly into place, as though pulled by two invisible hands.

Alvin Fernald, Great Inventor, had done it again.

Ten minutes later he was showing Shoie and the Pest his One-Jerk Bed Maker. They were so impressed they wanted to try the idea immediately on their own beds. Instead, Alvin insisted that they stay in his room for a very important conference.

He locked the door and turned on the Foolproof Burglar Alarm. After their latest adventure, he wanted no one to hear what they were discussing. They were about to make a big decision.

Alvin threw himself down on his pillow. The Pest and Shoie flopped down on the bed, too.

It was the first time, really, that his sister had been willingly included in the plans of the two boys. Somehow, it seemed natural to include her now. She was lying on top of his blanket on her stomach, her chin propped between her hands. Only once before had Alvin seen such a serious look on her face. That was the time she had climbed to the very top of the telephone pole out by Gilligan's pasture. Perched there, she had made the mistake of looking down. She'd grabbed the pole with both arms, but they'd had to call the ladder truck from the fire department to get her down. She'd been pretty serious after *that* episode, too.

It was no wonder that she was so serious. All three of them were, for they were faced with a big decision. What should they do about old Mrs. Huntley?

"Do you suppose she's still alive?" asked Shoie for the fourth time.

"I think she is," said Alvin. "I have a hunch she's still all right. Last night, when I was listening on the Eavesdropper, one of those men said, 'She's pretty smart.'

I'll bet he was talking about Mrs. Huntley. The reason I think she's still alive is that 'she is' is present tense."

"Present tents?" asked the Pest. "Present tents? Who's giving away tents, and what's that got to do with Mrs. Huntley?"

Alvin groaned. "Not present tents. Present *tense*. You wouldn't know anything about tense because you haven't been in Miss Riggs' room in school yet."

"Does she give away tents?" asked the Pest.

"Pretend I never mentioned it."

"I learned how to do timeses in school," offered the Pest.

"What do you mean — timeses?"

"You know — two times two is four, four times four is eight."

"What's that got to do with Mrs. Huntley? Besides, four times four is sixteen, not eight."

"So's two times eight."

"Who said it wasn't?"

"You did."

"Did not."

"Did so."

"Quit fighting, you two," said Shoie. "We've got to decide what we're going to do."

"Right, old bean. That's exactly what we have to do. Let's get down to business."

"If she's still alive," asked Shoie, "where is she? And is she in any danger?"

"I think I know where she is. I think she's in one of the towers of that old house. When I was on top of that fence last night I happened to look up at the tower on the left corner. There was a candle in the window."

"That's a spook," said the Pest. "Everybody knows that's the ghost of the old Huntley place."

"No. This wasn't a spook or a ghost. I saw somebody silhouetted at the window. I couldn't make out who it was, but I'll bet my next invention it was Mrs. Huntley."

The room was quiet for a moment. Shoie rolled over on his back, put his feet in the air, and started pedaling an imaginary bicycle upside down. The Mighty Athlete did this frequently to keep his legs in shape. Finally, he plopped them back down on the bed.

"Maybe we ought to tell Daddy," suggested the Pest for the third time.

"Maybe we ought," repeated Shoie.

"Maybe," said Alvin. "Then again, maybe not. Do we *know* anything is wrong over there? Do we *know* old Mrs. Huntley is in danger? Maybe those men are relatives. Maybe she invited them to visit her."

"Mommy told me once that she has only one living relative," said the Pest.

"Right. Her only relative is a nephew named Herbert. Maybe he's one of the men over there. And maybe he brought one of his friends along. Maybe they're just visiting, and nothing at all is wrong."

"If we told Daddy, he could arrest the men and find out who they are. He's the best policeman in the whole world."

"That's all the more reason why I don't want to tell Dad," said Alvin. "Do you remember last winter when Dad got in all that trouble? It wasn't his fault at all. Somebody broke into Mr. Peabody's store. Mr. Peabody

said he'd seen who it was — Mr. Riggs, who lives down by the tracks. Dad took Mr. Riggs down to the jail where he found out they'd already caught the real burglar. It wasn't Mr. Riggs at all, and was he hopping mad! He was going to sue Dad for ten thousand dollars for false arrest, or whatever they call it. Anyway, the Chief finally talked the man out of it. But you can't just go around arresting people. Even a policeman can't arrest people unless he *knows* they did something wrong, or at least it looks like they had committed a crime." Alvin paused for a minute. "Nope. I don't think we ought to tell Dad just yet. He might go over and arrest those men and get sued for a lot of money."

"I don't know," said Shoie doubtfully. "Maybe we ought to tell."

Alvin brought up his strongest argument. "If we tell," he said slowly. "Mom and Dad — and your parents too, Shoie — will know we've been sneaking around that old house. We'll really catch it then."

The other two thought about the consequences.

"Well, what are we going to do then?" asked Shoie.

"I'll tell you what we're going to do. We're going to find Mrs. Huntley and talk to her."

"We can't do that, Alvin," said the Pest. "We wouldn't dare sneak *inside* that old house."

"Count me out, and when you start counting, count me first," said Shoie.

"I think I know how we can talk to her without ever getting into the house."

Shoie and the Pest were astonished.

"What do you mean?" said Shoie. "Even Alvin Fernald isn't crazy enough to go over there and shout at her. At least I hope you aren't."

"Nope," said Alvin. He enjoyed mystifying them. "But I'll bet I can find out what's going on in there without those men knowing a thing about it."

"Bet you can't," said the Pest.

"How much will you bet?"

"Ten million dollars."

"How much do you have in your bank?"

"Eleven cents."

"Then," said Alvin, doing a little rapid calculating, "you're short only nine million, nine hundred and ninety-nine thousand, nine hundred and ninety-nine dollars and eighty-nine cents."

"I'll bet it anyway."

"You can't bet unless you have the money. Besides, the folks told us never to bet."

"I'll still bet you can't, Alvin. How could you do it?"

"With an invention."

"Watch it!" warned Shoie. "Your eyes are getting glassy again. You always go out of your head when you're thinking up a new invention."

It was true that Alvin was thinking furiously. Finally he said, "Will you try once more with me? Will you go over to that house right now if I promise that those men won't see you?"

"How can you promise that?" asked Shoie.

"I've invented an Invisible Powder," said Alvin. "You shake a little of it on you and you turn absolutely invisible. Just as though you aren't there."

The Pest's jaw dropped. "Alvin! Did you *really?*"

Alvin grinned at Shoie. "Yep. And any time you don't behave, Pest, I'll just sprinkle a little of it on you. Poof! You're gone!"

"Please don't do it, Alvin. I'll behave!"

Alvin smiled. "You'd believe anything, wouldn't you? No, I haven't really invented an Invisible Powder. But if I promise that you won't be seen, will you go over to the old house with me?"

"I guess so," said the Pest.

Shoie couldn't stand for a girl to be braver than he was. He finally agreed to go along. "But you have to promise one thing, Alvin. If we find out something *is* wrong over there, or if we don't see Mrs. Huntley, then we go straight to your dad and tell him everything."

"It's a bargain." Alvin thought for a minute. "Now we have to get the parts for the Jet Powered Message Carrier. Shoie, it's a good thing you were the best bow and arrow shooter in our grade last year. I want you to get your bow and some arrows, and meet us at the corner. Pest, you get a pencil, some pieces of paper and Dad's fishing reel. Don't let Mom see you take the reel. Bring along a paper sack. I'll get the other stuff myself."

"Here we go again," groaned Shoie. "Okay. I'll meet you at the corner in five minutes."

Chapter 8

THE JET-POWERED MESSAGE CARRIER

Hi, Robin Hood," said Alvin with a grin as Shoie showed up, the bow slung across his shoulder, a quiver full of arrows on his back.

"All set," said Shoie.

Alvin was carrying a paper sack. He handed it to the Pest. "Here, you're the carrier. Hang this around your neck and pretend you're a St. Bernard."

The Pest looked puzzled. "What's a St. Bernard, Alvin?"

"It's a big dog that carries medicine and stuff to people lost in the mountains. As long as you're the St. Bernard, let's hear you bark."

She didn't know whether he was kidding or not. "*Rowf!*" she said. "*Rowf! Rowf!*"

Alvin and Shoie kept straight faces.

"That's pretty good," said Alvin, "but you really should bark louder if you're going to be the St. Bernard on *this* expedition. Try it again."

"*Rowf! Rowf!*"

"That's better. Okay, you can come along. But don't bark unless I tell you to."

"How do I hang this sack around my neck?"

Alvin and Shoie looked at each other and started to laugh. Finally Alvin reached out and mussed up her hair. It was the only way he had ever found to show her that he liked her. For as long as he could remember she had been tagging after him, always getting in the way. So, once in a while when he *did* want to say something nice to her, he didn't know how. Whenever he wanted to show that he really liked her, he mussed up her hair. He knew she liked it, even though she pretended she didn't.

"We were only kidding. You make a wonderful St. Bernard, but don't work too hard at it. Just carry the sack for us. I hope I haven't forgotten anything."

This time Alvin led them clear over to Hickory Street, then circled around so they could come up on the old Huntley place from the rear. The back end of the lot was covered with even more trees and bushes than the front. Standing beside the iron fence, they couldn't even see the house except for one of the towers, so they knew they couldn't be seen either.

They climbed the fence and dropped inside. Alvin put a finger to his lips and sneaked off through the weeds like the jungle fighters in the movies. The others were following. He moved from bush to bush and tree to tree, always keeping something between himself and the old house. At last he stopped behind a clump of bushes. Through the branches they could see the corner of the house with the tower rising high into the air.

The three sank down to the soft ground.

"That's the tower where I saw the candle," whispered Alvin. "And I'll bet old Mrs. Huntley is up there."

"Look," said Shoie. "The window's open. But I don't see anything of her."

"Don't see her," echoed the Pest.

"Well, that doesn't mean she isn't there."

"How are you going to talk to her without letting those bad men know about it?" asked the Pest.

"A lot of it will be up to you, Shoie," said Alvin. "Now we've got to get ready. Give me your bow."

Shoie handed him the bow. From the paper sack Alvin took his dad's fishing reel, some short pieces of wire, and a pair of pliers. He showed Shoie how to hold the reel tight against the handle of the bow, and he wrapped the wire around the projections on the reel. With the pliers he twisted the wire tight so the reel was held firmly in place.

From the paper sack Alvin took a pencil and a pad of paper. On the top sheet he wrote the following message:

Dear Mrs. Huntley,

If you are in the tower, and if you need help, please let me know by pulling twice on the fishing line. Then tie the line to something near the window. Another message will follow.

A Bird Lover

"There," he said. "That ought to do the job." He took one of the arrows from the quiver on Shoie's back. He wrapped the message carefully around it near the feathers, fastening it in place with some tape from the paper sack. Then he took his knife from his pocket.

"Sorry, old bean," he said, looking up at Shoie, "but I've got to do this." With the knife he cut a ring just behind the arrowhead. Pulling a little fishing line out

of the reel, he wrapped the end of it around the notch and tied it tightly.

"There," he said, admiring the neatness of his work. "Okay, Robin Hood. It's up to you. Do you think you can shoot the arrow through that window in the tower?"

Shoie gazed up at the window. He closed one eye as though he were aiming. "Maybe I can," he said. "I'll give it a try."

The Mighty Athlete crawled to his feet and sighted this way and that through the bush. Finally, he said, "I think this is the best place."

Alvin handed him the bow. "Don't miss. If we make much of a racket, those two men are liable to come running out here. Pest, you stay down behind the bush. If anything happens, you run just as fast as you can. Don't wait for us. Just run on home."

Shoie dropped to one knee and put the arrow in place on the bow. He pulled back the bow as far as he could. For a long moment he sighted, holding his breath, then released the arrow.

Whaaaaaannnng!

"Ohmigosh," whispered Alvin, "I forgot to take the clicker off the fishing reel."

The reel made an awful racket as the line went out. And the clicker pulled back on the line so much that the arrow didn't even reach the house, let alone the high tower. The three crouched low behind the bush.

Finally Shoie whispered, "I guess they didn't hear anything inside. What do we do now?"

Alvin began pulling on the fishing line to retrieve the arrow. "Start reeling in the line," he directed. The arrow came snaking back through the weeds toward them. Finally they could reach it. Shoie put it in the bow once more, and they were ready to give it another try. This time Alvin remembered to take the clicker off the reel.

It was a strong bow, and Shoie pulled it back just as far as he could. He took careful aim, then released the arrow. He held his breath as it soared through the air, the line zipping out of the reel. It looked as if the arrow would go straight through the window. Then, at the last instant, it began wobbling as though caught in a sudden breeze. It hit just beside the window with a thud, and fell to the ground.

With a sigh Alvin reached for the reel and started winding in the line again.

"Look!" said the Pest. "Look! There's somebody at the window."

Sure enough, a face had appeared at the open window, the wrinkled face of an old woman.

"It's her," whispered Alvin. "It's Mrs. Huntley."

"At least we know she's safe," whispered Shoie.

Alvin wound in the line as fast as he dared. The kindly old face peered down, looking all around the yard, but they knew from her expression that she hadn't spotted them.

At last they were ready to try once more. Shoie pulled back on the bow and sighted carefully along the arrow. Suddenly he eased off the pressure and pointed the arrow at the ground.

"Gosh," he said, "what if I hit her?"

Alvin thought for a minute. "I guess we'll just have

to take a chance those two men aren't watching. I'm going out there where she'll see me. Maybe I can get her to move away from the window." He crawled around the bush until he was kneeling in front of it. Looking up at the window, he waved his arm.

Mrs. Huntley, peering down at the ground, suddenly saw him. She waved back. Then she did a strange thing. She put a finger to her lips and motioned with her other hand for him to go away.

Alvin kept right on waving furiously, trying to get her to move away from the window. The more he waved, the more she waved. He didn't dare take a chance on calling to her. Finally he crawled back.

"Shoie," he said, "you've got to crawl out there and aim at her. Really pretend you're going to shoot. Maybe then she'll get away from the window. But don't shoot that arrow if you can see her. We don't want to take a chance on hurting her.

Shoie looked doubtful. "What if they're watching from the house? What if they have a gun?"

"I was out there, wasn't I? Nobody hurt me, did they? Just do as I say, then get back here behind the bush as fast as you can."

Shoie took a long look at the window, then crawled out into the open. He put the arrow in the bow, drew back and aimed directly at the face in the window.

Old Mrs. Huntley looked scared. She stared down at Shoie, then disappeared.

"Fire!" hissed Alvin. "Fire!"

The arrow left the bow cleanly, trailing the fine fishing line. It arched through the air, climbing higher and higher. With a flash it disappeared into the room. Shoie dived back behind the bush.

They waited. Nothing happened. They waited what seemed to be an hour. Finally Shoie, still holding the bow, felt two jerks on the line. Alvin reached out and pulled cautiously on the line until it was taut.

"Good!" he said. "She read the message and tied the line inside." He handed the line to the Pest. "Hold this tight," he said. "Now it's time for step number two — the Jet-Powered Message Carrier."

From the paper sack he took a strange little rig. The main part was a piece of light wood. Taped to the bottom of it was a little aluminum cylinder. And screwed into the top were two tiny hooks.

"What's that?" whispered Shoie.

"Don't you recognize it? This little aluminum thing is the jet engine off my model plane. I rigged it up as a message carrier. Give me the paper and pencil."

On a slip of paper Alvin wrote the second message:

Dear Mrs. Huntley,

Attached is a piece of a pencil. Use it to write a message on the back of this paper. We want to know whether you are in any danger. If you are, we will call the police. My dad is the best policeman in town. When you have written your message, use the tape to fasten it to this jet engine. Hook the engine back on the fishing line and give it a little shove. It will coast back down to us.

Another Bird Lover

Alvin broke the tip off the pencil and carefully folded it inside the paper. "Got to save weight," he whispered. "I can't send the whole pencil." He taped the message to the jet engine and placed the two hooks over the line so the Jet Message Carrier hung below.

On his model plane the jet engine worked fine. He hoped it would work as well on this invention. Protruding from the back of the engine was a tiny fuse. From the sack he took some wooden matches. He tried lighting one of the matches on the seat of his pants, the way Dad struck a match sometimes. He broke six matches before he finally gave up, reached over, and struck another on Shoie's belt buckle. He touched the flame to the fuse.

The fuse sputtered as the flame burned up into the engine. Then,

Whooooooooosh!

The Jet Message Carrier hung there motionless for a moment, as though gathering its energy. Then it started moving slowly up the fishing line. The farther it went, the faster it went, and by the time it disappeared into the window it was moving so fast it was nothing but a silver flash.

"Worked!" said Alvin excitedly. "My Jet-Powered Message Carrier worked."

"What next?" asked Shoie.

"We wait for an answer."

"What if those men see the fishing line?"

"That's the chance we'll have to take. But that's mighty light line. It would take a sharp eye to see it."

Lying on their stomachs behind the bush, they waited.

The Pest was holding the fishing line tight. At last it began to tremble. They looked up and saw the Message Carrier coasting down toward them.

Alvin caught the Carrier and ripped off the message. He unfolded it, his hands shaking a little. He hoped it would solve the mystery of the old house. The message was scrawled in a trembling hand, and some of the letters were difficult to make out. It said:

> Please PLEASE don't call the police. I am in danger, but I do not want the police. There are two men inside the house. If you can figure out any way to do it, please get the men away from the house, but do not put yourselves in any danger. And DON'T CALL THE POLICE.
>
> I remember one of you boys. You helped me feed my birds. If you can't do anything else, please feed my birds just as soon as possible. By now Mr. Huntley will be very hungry.

"She doesn't make sense," said Shoie. "She's crazy, all right. First she says she's in danger, then she says not to call the police."

"I think we ought to tell Daddy," said the Pest.

Alvin was lost in thought. Finally, he took the cover off the jet engine and put in some more of the pellets that made it go. He inserted a new piece of fuse and snapped the cover back in place. With the Jet Message Carrier ready, he wrote:

> Dear Mrs. Huntley,
>
> Don't worry about your birds. We will see

that they are fed. And we won't call the police.
I plan to capture the two men myself. I am an
inventor. I will figure out an invention to
capture them. All of my inventions work. So
don't worry about a thing. We will see you
soon. Untie the fish line.

> Alvin Fernald,
> Great Inventor and
> Bird Lover.

Once more the Jet Message Carrier zoomed up the
fish line and disappeared in the window. A couple of
minutes later the line went slack in the Pest's hand, and
came fluttering to the ground.

"You see?" said Alvin. "She has more faith in me
than you two. She knows I'll help her out." He reeled
up the fishing line and handed Shoie the bow. Picking
up the paper sack, he handed it to the Pest. "Let's get
out of here before we're discovered."

"*Rowf!*" said the Pest softly, a grin on her face.

Chapter 9

ALVIN was so excited he could scarcely eat his lunch. When Alvin couldn't eat, it meant one of two things. Either he was inventing or, as his mother would say, he was "coming down with something." This noon, Mom and Dad kept telling him to eat, but it was difficult for him to bring his thoughts back to the plate in front of him. Mom didn't notice the glassy look in his eye or she would have known he was inventing. She made him promise not to run and get hot that afternoon. Dad told him to lie down after lunch, which was exactly what Alvin wanted to do.

For half an hour Alvin lay on his bed, thinking furiously. Sometimes when he was inventing he thought so hard it scared him. This was one of those times. Finally, he got up and rummaged through his bench until he found a pencil and paper. For another thirty minutes he sat there, carefully drawing a map of the high fence, the yard, and the old Huntley house. When he had finished the map he started writing notes on it, drawing arrows pointing to certain spots.

The more he worked, the more excited he became. This, he decided, would be the greatest invention of his life. Why, it would probably make him famous.

On another sheet of paper he made a long list of things he would need for his invention. He tucked the

list into the pocket of his shirt. After studying the map once more, he tore it into tiny bits and hid it in the bottom of the wastebasket. Once on television he'd seen a spy swallow a piece of paper with a secret code on it. Somehow Alvin wasn't very hungry for a paper map, but he didn't want to leave any evidence around.

At last he hollered down the stairway for his sister. She came bouncing up, her eyes wide with excitement.

"Go call Shoie," he said, "and have him meet us behind the garage in five minutes."

"What are you going to do, Alvin?"

"Don't ask questions. Just get Shoie. Tell him we're going to have a supersecret council meeting."

"Can I come, too?"

" 'Course you can — if you don't tell anybody else about it."

They met in the warm sun behind the garage. First Alvin took from his pocket the note that old Mrs. Huntley had written.

"Now read this again," he said, "and see what you make of it."

Shoie read it over. "I think she's crazy, like everybody says."

"What makes you say that?"

"Well, first she says not to call the police. Then she says she's in danger. Just doesn't make sense."

"But couldn't it be true?" asked Alvin. "Couldn't she be in danger and still not want the police? I can think of at least three reasons why she might act this way."

"I can't even think of one," said the Pest.

"In the first place," explained Alvin, "she might be doing something herself in that old house that she doesn't want the police to find out about. She might be breaking the law some way herself."

"In that case," said Shoie, "it's our duty to tell the police."

"Right. But I don't think she's breaking the law. She's too nice an old lady. I just mentioned it as a possibility. An inventor analyzes everything, you know. Now here's another reason she might be acting that way. Maybe she *is* kind of crazy, but in a harmless sort of a way. She's been living all alone in that house for a good many years. By now, maybe, she doesn't trust anybody. Maybe the old story is true. Maybe she has a lot of money hidden in that house, and she doesn't trust even the police for fear they'll take it away."

"She trusts you," said the Pest. "She trusts you or she wouldn't have asked you to help."

"That's because she thinks I'm another bird lover."

"Oh."

"There's a third reason she might not want us to call the police. Her note proves that she's afraid of those two men. But suppose, even though she's afraid of them, that she wants to protect one or both of them."

"Why in the world would she want to do that?" asked Shoie.

"Well, suppose you had only one relative in the world. And suppose that relative were bad, bad enough to threaten you. Even though he did something bad, you might still want to protect him, mightn't you?"

"Maybe," said the Pest doubtfully.

"Now you're beginning to make sense," said Shoie excitedly. "You think one of those men is her nephew."

"Right. At least that's a possible answer."

"Don't you think we ought to tell your dad?"

"No," said Alvin. "No, I don't. I promised her I wouldn't call the police. Besides, there's no need to call them." He paused for a moment, to emphasize his next words. "There's no need to call the police because *I'm going to capture those two men myself.*"

"You're out of your mind," said Shoie. "All that inventing has affected your brain. How could you capture two grown men?"

"I can capture them. I'll do it with an invention I've worked out."

"Fooey," said Shoie. "I don't believe it."

"Would it be dangerous?" asked the Pest.

"Maybe. And I'd need your help."

"Would it make us famous?" asked Shoie.

"Sure would."

Shoie and the Pest looked at each other. Finally Shoie said, "Let's hear your plan."

Alvin knew they'd never join him if he told them all he planned to do. "Nope. Either you trust my inventions or you don't. I've invented an Automatic Man Trap. You'll have to take my word that it will work."

"Your inventions always work," said the Pest.

"We have only a few hours to rig up this trap, so we'd better get busy. First we'll need the parts to make the invention. I have a list here."

He pulled the piece of paper out of his pocket. The list read:

Fireplace bellows	Pulley
Popcorn	Gunny sacks
Pepper	Hammer
Long rope	Nails
Several short ropes	Shovel
Strong string	Knife

"Pest," he said, "you try to sneak out the fireplace bellows — that thing with the long snout that blows air onto the fire. On your way through the house bring out that big bag of unpopped popcorn and the can of pepper."

"Fireplace bellows, popcorn, and pepper," repeated the Pest. "You sure you know what you're doing, Alvin?"

"Sure. Now run. Shoie, you go over to your house and bring back three or four of those gunny sacks I've seen in your basement. You know, those big cloth bags."

"Check, old man," said Shoie.

"I'll go up to the room and take apart my Portable Fire Escape so I can use the long rope and one of the pulleys. And I'll bring the hammer and nails. We can get the other stuff out of the garage. Okay. Let's go. We'll meet back here."

A few minutes later, three figures sneaked down the alley to avoid being seen. Once more they went all the way around by Hickory Street so they could approach the house from the rear. They sauntered along the sidewalk beside the iron fence.

Alvin looked up and down the street. "Now!" he said.

They poked the stuff for the Automatic Man Trap between the bars and managed to get over the fence without being seen.

"Come on," said Alvin. "And keep quiet. If we're real careful, we can stay hidden in the trees and bushes so nobody can see us from the house or street."

They sneaked around the house until they were close to the front, hidden from the porch only by some low branches. Alvin signaled the others to stop.

"How does your invention work?" asked the Pest in a low voice.

"No time for questions. Here, give me the bellows and the pepper," he ordered. He pumped the bellows once or twice, and listened to the air rush out the long snout. Through a hole in the back end of the bellows he carefully poured the entire can of pepper.

"There. That part's ready. Now untie the string around that bag of popcorn so we can get at it without any trouble."

Shoie untied the string and handed the bag to Alvin.

"We'll leave these things right here beside this rock," said Alvin softly, covering the bellows and the bag of popcorn with weeds. "You'll have to help me find them later, so remember where they are, Pest."

"I'll remember," said his sister.

"The next part's lots harder. Come on. We've got to find a tree not far from the porch, but still hidden."

Alvin crept through the wooded yard, looking up at the trees. Shoie and the Pest did the same thing, even though they didn't know what they were looking for.

Finally, Alvin chose a big tree with a strong branch that hung out toward the house. He squinted this way and that. "They can't see us from the house," he said. "This tree should be fine. Do you think you can climb it, oh Mighty Athlete?"

"In my sleep," said Shoie.

Alvin handed him the pulley and a short piece of rope. "Climb out on the limb and tie on the pulley. Tie it on good and tight."

Shoie did as he was told. When the pulley was in place, Alvin tossed one end of the long rope to him. "Put that through the pulley and drop it back down," he said in a low voice.

A moment later the rope ran up, over the pulley, and back down to the ground again. Shoie slid down, and the three of them squatted beneath the branch.

"Now," said Alvin, "some way or other we've got to get two hundred pounds of weight up on that tree limb and fastened there. I'll tell you how we're going to do it. The ground over there by those bushes is mostly sand. We'll use one of the bags to drag over some sand, a little at a time, until we have two of the other bags filled."

It took quite awhile, and a good many trips to fill the bags beneath the trees.

"There," said Alvin, the sweat running down his face. "I figure each of those bags must weigh close to a hundred pounds." He tied one end of the long rope around the top of one of the bags. "Now we'll all pull the other end together and get the bag up to the branch."

They grabbed the other end of the rope and pulled. The heavy bag rose slowly, higher and higher, until it touched the branch. They tied the other end of the rope around a little tree nearby to keep the bag from coming back down.

Alvin handed Shoie a short piece of rope. "Now shinny back up there and tie that bag to the branch," he said. "Then untie the long rope and come back down so we can haul up the other bag."

"Seems like a lot of trouble to me," said Shoie as he started up the tree again. Crawling out on the branch, he began working with the ropes.

"About ready?" called Alvin.

"I've tied the bag to the branch, but I haven't got the long rope untied yet," said Shoie.

"Keep working," ordered Alvin. He went over and untied the other end of the long rope from the little

tree. Now there was no pull against it. He brought it back beneath the branch.

Suddenly it happened.

"Look out!" called down Shoie, his voice rising a little. The knot in the short rope was slipping.

The heavy bag swung free. Alvin was still hanging onto the other end of the rope, and he found himself sailing up toward the tree branch. Just as he bonked his head against the branch, the bag hit the ground with a thud. The bottom of the bag broke, and the sand spilled out. Now, just as suddenly, Alvin found himself sailing back down as the empty bag whistled

up toward the pulley. Alvin hit the ground with a crash, and let loose of the rope. Immediately, the empty bag came sailing back down and landed on his head, draping itself across his shoulders.

For a moment Shoie looked down, speechless. Then he said softly, "Wow! That looked like fun, Alvin! Can I try it?"

Alvin staggered to his feet. He was mad clear through. "Good gosh, can't you even tie a knot?" One at a time he shook his arms and legs to make sure nothing was broken. At last he said, "Come on back down. Now we've got to do the whole thing over again."

It took them two hours to finish the Automatic Man Trap. One at a time, they hauled two heavy bags of sand up into the tree and tied them.

Now Shoie was perched on the branch.

"Tie the rope that goes through the pulley to both of the bags," ordered Alvin.

This time Shoie did a good tight job with the knots.

Alvin tossed up a ball of heavy cord. "You've got to bind that rope to the branch with this cord," he said. "It's got to be strong enough to hold the bags up there, but we've got to be able to cut the cord real quick with a knife."

Shoie did as he was told.

"Okay," said Alvin. "Now untie the short ropes and come on down here."

Shoie jumped lightly to the ground, and the three stood looking up at the Automatic Man Trap. The long rope ran up and over the pulley and was tied to the two heavy bags. A string bound the rope to the branch so the bags couldn't fall.

The loose end of the long rope was on the ground. Alvin picked it up.

"Now," he said, "we'll practice what we're going to do tonight."

Chapter 10

THE BIGGEST ADVENTURE OF ALL

FOR the fourth time, the three figures crept toward the house.

The Pest hoped it would be the last time. It was different, now, because they weren't just spying. They were trying to capture the two men inside.

Shoie had the feeling he was on a big train roaring off into the night. He couldn't stop the train and he couldn't get off. He was scared, but somehow he knew that he couldn't stop now.

Alvin was more excited than he had ever been in his life. His heart was beating so loudly that he was sure it could be heard even inside the house. For the first time since they had started prowling around the old Huntley place, he wasn't a bit scared — just excited. He had developed a great invention to trap two men he believed to be criminals. Nothing could stop him from trying his master plan now.

In the dim moonlight Daphne suddenly moved her hand toward her nose.

"Alvin," she said in a strangled voice. "Alvin, I'm going to sneeze!"

"Don't you dare!" he growled, suddenly aware that a simple little sneeze could ruin his plan.

"*Ugggl — ugggle —*" The Pest was making strange noises. Then, "*Ugggl — SHISSSSSSSSH!*"

He grabbed her nose too late. The sneeze sounded like an explosion in the still night air. They crouched there in the weeds near the porch, motionless. It seemed that hours passed. No one dared move.

At last Alvin raised his head and peered toward the dimly lighted room. There, silhouetted against the glass, was the figure of a man staring out at them.

Alvin could feel the tingle crawl up his spine. Though he couldn't see the man's eyes, he was sure they were staring directly at him.

He kept his head up, not daring to drop back down into the weeds.

"*Ugggl — ugggle!*"

The Pest was going to sneeze again.

At that moment the figure walked away from the window. Alvin reached down and clamped his hand across the Pest's face.

"*Shisssssssh!*" This time the sneeze was more of a whisper than an explosion.

For a long time they crouched there in the grass. At last Alvin saw shadows move across the window again. He had the feeling that the two men inside were resuming their search.

"Let's go," he whispered. He felt the Pest shaking beside him. "You scared?"

"S-s-scared?" she repeated. "You b-b-b-bet!"

"Well, don't ruin everything now. We'll do it, just as we practiced it this afternoon." He turned to Shoie. "Are you ready, old man?"

"I dunno," whispered Shoie. "I guess so."

"Okay. Here's the knife. To your post. And good luck!"

Shoie took the knife and sneaked away through the long grass.

Alvin and the Pest crawled through the weeds toward the place where they had hidden the bellows and the popcorn. Now, in the darkness, nothing looked the same. He couldn't seem to find the right rock. As time passed he grew frantic. And as he searched, he had the horrifying thought that the men inside had found the bellows and knew exactly what he was doing at this moment.

He went back over the same ground, then crawled on a little farther. Now he felt a rock that seemed to be about the right size. As he searched, he leaned against the rock, and suddenly it toppled over. He reached out an arm to recover his balance, and his hand went right on down into a hole in the ground, a hole that had been covered by the rock. His fingers touched something that wasn't dirt. It was some sort of a box, with a loose lid. He lifted the lid, reached inside, and immediately felt something crinkly.

A paper bag!

Instantly Alvin knew what it was. He jerked back his hand as though he'd touched a piece of red-hot metal. Then his hand went back into the hole, and he felt the bag once more.

"What's the matter, Alvin?" asked the Pest.

"Ssssh!"

Alvin withdrew his hand. He didn't want to say

anything about the paper bag to his sister just yet. He crawled on a little farther, searching, and at last found the bellows and the bag of popcorn.

"Got it." He handed her the popcorn.

The Pest hung back as they crawled up the rickety porch steps. He had to reach back and pull her onto the porch floor beside him. He knew she was more scared than she had ever been in her life as she lay there looking up at him. Alvin reached out and put his arm around her. He squeezed her tight.

"Too scared?" he whispered into her ear. "Want to go home, Daphne? I'll take you home."

She looked up at him. Her eyes were almost as big as her face. "Oh, Alvin," she whispered. "That's the first time you ever called me Daphne instead of the Pest."

"Do what you're supposed to do, then *run just as fast as you can.*"

Bravely, she crawled over and stood up beside the door. In her hands was the open bag of popcorn.

Alvin sneaked across the porch. He leaned against the railing. He was holding the handles of the bellows.

He stood there for a moment, his feet spread wide apart. This was the moment he had planned for. Now, for the first time that night, he was scared. He wondered if they shouldn't leave as quietly as they had come, sneak home and get Dad.

No! He had promised Mrs. Huntley he'd help her. And he'd bragged that all his inventions worked.

Alvin lifted his head. He shouted, "Hey in there!" His voice faded off into the stillness of the night.

There was a scuffling noise inside the house. The

door burst open so suddenly that it swung on around and almost hit the Pest in the face. One of the men, the one with the thin face, leaped through the doorway. He looked around the porch until he could see Alvin.

"I'll get you this time!" he said in a low voice.

Alvin watched the man jump across the porch toward him. He waited until the very last moment, then swung up the bellows and pumped it as hard as he could into the man's face. Air hissed through the snout.

The man stopped as though he'd been hit by a brick. His face half-covered with pepper, he gasped for breath. His eyes were closed and he staggered blindly backward.

"The popcorn!" shouted Alvin.

The Pest gave a mighty heave of the bag, and the popcorn spilled out across the porch floor. As the man staggered backward, his shoes hit the hard, round little kernels. His feet flew out from under him. As he fell, his head hit the porch railing. He was unconscious even before he hit the floor.

At that instant the second man burst through the door. Within two steps he, too, hit the popcorn and his feet flew toward the sky. For a moment he lay there moaning. Then he spotted the Pest crouching nearby. She had been too horrified to move.

"Run!" shouted Alvin. "Run, Pest, run!"

The man reached a long arm toward her. His fingers brushed her sleeve. Then she was dashing down the steps and diving into the bushes.

Alvin vaulted over the porch railing and ran around in front of the steps. He stood there, heart pounding. The man was glaring down at him.

"I'll get you meddling kids," growled the man. "I'll get you if it's the last thing I do!" Then he was on his feet, ready to leap off the steps.

For a fraction of a second the magnificent brain stopped functioning. Then Alvin ran — ran for his life. His legs felt as though they were made of lead, and just behind him he could hear the whistle of the man's breath.

When Alvin reached the tree he was two steps ahead of the man. He stopped suddenly and turned, the bellows in front of his chest. For just a fraction of a second the man hesitated, peering down to see what Alvin held in his hands.

"Now, Shoie!"

There was just one movement, a very slight one, on the branch above.

It was an amazing sight. One moment Alvin was standing there staring at the man. An instant later there was a whistling sound from above as the two hundred pounds of sand came plummeting down. At the same instant the man's feet were jerked out from under him and he vanished, shoes first.

Shoie dropped beside Alvin with a thud. For long seconds they stared up in awe at what they had done. The man was hanging by his feet, which were tightly bound in the noose Alvin had concealed in the grass. His arms were waving wildly and he was shouting at the top of his voice.

"Gosh," Alvin said in a low voice. "It worked."

Shoie was speechless. All he could do was stand there and stare.

Alvin knew they still had work to do. "Come on, Shoie. We've got to make sure the other one doesn't wake up and get away."

Back at the house, they peered cautiously across the porch. The man was still lying on his back, motionless.

"Quick, get the rest of the Automatic Man Trap," ordered Alvin as he ran over beside the man.

The rest of the Trap consisted of the hammer and nails. Quickly, Alvin went to work. He put one nail through the sleeve of the man's jacket and hammered it into the floorboard. He did the same with the other sleeve, then nailed down each trouser leg.

Alvin was afraid the man would wake up before he finished, so he worked as fast as he could. Five minutes later, when the man opened his eyes, his clothing was securely nailed to the floor. In fact, he was framed with nails. When he raised his head and tried to get up, he couldn't move a muscle. He gazed down at his arms and legs, eyes bulging.

But Alvin didn't trust the nails in the rotten floorboards. Just as the man opened his mouth to speak, Alvin pumped the bellows to give him another snort of pepper. The man gasped once, and his head hit the floor with a thud.

Out in the tree, the other man was still thrashing and shouting.

"Pest," called Alvin. "Pest, are you still there?"

She came slowly up the steps. Her eyes were shining. "Oh, Alvin," she said. "Oh, Alvin, you're so brave. And your invention worked just like you said it would."

"Of course it did," said Alvin. "All my inventions

work." Suddenly he remembered. "But we don't have time to stand around here talking about my inventions. We have to find old Mrs. Huntley."

"Gee!" said Shoie. "I almost forgot all about her."

"Follow me."

Alvin opened the front door and walked into the house. In the front room a candle was burning in an old-fashioned candlestick. He picked it up and led the way over to a doorway that opened into a hall. They were standing at the bottom of a long flight of stairs.

Up the steps went the three figures, huddled together in the flickering light, until they reached a long balcony overlooking the hall. Four doors opened off the balcony. One by one they swung open three of the doors, then closed them again on bedrooms filled with dusty old-fashioned furniture. The fourth door opened on narrow, steep stairs that wound up into the darkness above. They crept up the steps. Even though they knew the danger now was past, they couldn't help feeling scared in the eerie house. It was almost as though the ghost of the old Huntley place were waiting for them at the top of the stairway.

Instead of a ghost, they found a closed door blocking the steps. Alvin tried the doorknob. The door was locked, but there was a key beneath the knob. He turned the key, then pushed open the door. It creaked on rusty old hinges.

The room was tiny, with a single window on one wall. Seated by the window was Mrs. Huntley, her wrinkled face lighted by a candle on a table in front of her. When they entered she had a frightened look on her

face, but as soon as she saw Alvin in the doorway the
fear melted into a gentle smile.

Her first words came as a surprise. Alvin expected
her to say something about the two men down below.

"Did you feed my birds?" she asked quietly.

"N-n-not yet," stammered Alvin. "But we will, as
soon as it's daylight."

"You are a good boy," she said. "I knew you would
come for me. But please take care of my birds. I — I'm
not very strong any more, and I may have trouble getting
down those stairs to put out the feed. I've been locked
up here for five days." She seemed to want to talk about
herself, as though she'd been lonesome for a very long
time. "I'm getting old, you know, and forgetful. Oh, I

never forget to feed my birds. But I forget lots of other things. I can't even remember important things any-more, can't remember where I put things at all. I can't remember where I put my money, so how could I tell them what they wanted to know?" She shook her head slowly. "My goodness, Mr. Huntley will be so very hungry."

"You don't have to be afraid of the men downstairs any more, Mrs. Huntley," said Alvin. "We captured them with my inventions."

"I'm glad," she said. "But you must let them go, you know. You must let them go after they've promised not to bother me anymore."

Alvin was stunned. "But Mrs. Huntley! We can't let them go! They might lock us all up here. And — and — well, who'd feed the birds then?" he finished lamely.

At that instant a door slammed downstairs. Then they heard the sound of running feet.

"Yeeow!" shouted the Pest. "They're loose! They're coming after us!"

Alvin was so scared he dropped his candle. It went out before it struck the floor. They stood there motion-less in the flickering light of the single candle on the table by the window.

Now they could hear feet pounding up the steps and running along the balcony. Doors slammed. Then the footsteps came slowly up the narrow stairs to the tower. The Pest stood by Mrs. Huntley, eyes wide, her hand over her mouth.

Alvin went into action. He hurled himself across the

room and swung the door. He had just a glimpse of a beam of light on the steps below before he slammed the door. The knob turned slowly, and someone pushed against the door. Alvin was shoved into the room. Then the light was shining in his face.

"Alvin! Alvin, what are you doing here? And you, Daphne — and Shoie? What's all this about?" It was Dad's voice. Never had it sounded so good.

The Pest, who had been huddled in the corner, raced across the room and threw herself into Dad's arms. She was crying.

Alvin heard other voices downstairs. "Dad, there are two bad men down there. Don't let them get away."

"Don't worry about those two men," said Dad. "They'll never get away. They were mighty helpless when we found them. There are four other officers down there taking care of them. Come on, let's go downstairs. I want to find out what's going on in this house."

"But Mrs. Huntley," said Alvin. "She's too weak to get down the steps."

Dad went over and looked straight into the old lady's eyes. "It's good to see you again, Mrs. Huntley. Don't you worry about a thing. I'm going to take these children downstairs. Just as soon as I get down there, I'll send up two strong men to carry you down. Don't you worry."

A powerful light had been brought from a squad car and was shining on the front porch. One of the officers had recovered the man from the tree. The man was sitting on the steps, his eyes bulging, still gasping for breath.

Another officer was working over the other man. "Say," he called, tugging at the man's clothing, trying to rip it loose, "this isn't a bad invention. Maybe we should use it instead of handcuffs. Looks like it will take me fifteen minutes, just to pry this fellow loose from the floor."

Two officers came through the front door carrying Mrs. Huntley between them.

"We're taking her to the hospital," said one of them. "She's badly in need of medical care."

Mrs. Huntley looked Alvin squarely in the face. A single tear — a tear of gratitude — rolled from one of her eyes, down her face, then disappeared in a deep wrinkle.

"Don't forget," she said. "Please don't forget to take care of my birds."

Chapter 11

THE REWARD

ALVIN awoke with a start, sensing that something was different. Suddenly he knew what it was. The Silent Waker Upper had failed to jerk his toe and the sun was slanting through the window from high in the morning sky. He looked at the clock. Wow! He was already an hour late in delivering the morning papers.

He leaped out of bed and climbed into his clothes. He was in such a hurry that he didn't even wash his face before he dashed downstairs. Dad was sitting at the breakfast table.

"Hello, Alvin," he said. "Sit down and have some breakfast. I want to talk to you."

"Can't." Alvin headed for the front door. "Already late for my paper route. See you later, Dad."

"Come back here, Alvin." Something in Dad's voice stopped him. "Don't worry about your paper route. We figured you needed some sleep. I turned off your alarm last night after you were in bed, and your mother insisted on delivering your papers this morning. She should be back any minute now."

Alvin looked out the front door. His mother was riding his bicycle down the street. And just as he watched, she pulled the special release trigger. The last paper sailed through the air and landed smack on the top step of Mrs. Perkins' house.

When Mom walked into the house she was out of breath. "Say, Alvin," she said, a surprised tone in her voice, "that invention of yours works fine. Sort of fun, too. May I try it again sometime?"

"Sure, Mom." Alvin grinned.

The Pest walked into the room, rubbing sleep out of her eyes. "Can I try it too, Alvin?"

"No!" he snapped. Suddenly he remembered how brave she'd been last night. "Well, maybe. We'll see whether you can reach the pedals on my bike."

"Sit down, children," said Dad. "I want to talk to you about last night. It was too late to get the whole story from you then. Now, Alvin, I want you to start at the beginning and tell me everything."

Half an hour later, Alvin was still talking. He described the whole adventure, from the time the paper sailed through the air and crashed through the window of the old Huntley place. At one point he said, "Gosh, and a mirror from your purse is in that Electric Periscope, Mom." Later he suddenly remembered something else. "And our hose — I mean my Supersecret Eavesdropper — is still lying on the ground." Finally he finished the story. ". . . and then you and the squad car came, and took the two men off to the police station. How did you know we were there, Dad?"

"Someone was walking past, heard some yelling and thrashing around in a tree, and called the station."

"Oh. We sure were glad to see you."

Dad looked at him sternly. Then he turned and looked at the Pest. It was the sort of a look Dad always got just before he punished them.

Finally he said, "Both of you should be spanked within an inch of your lives. In the first place, you've been told many times to stay away from the Huntley house. In the second place, Alvin, you sawed off your mother's broom handle, took one of her mirrors, and used the garden hose without permission. In the third place, both of you sneaked out at night. We want no sneaks in this family. In the fourth place, you know better than to take the chances you did with two dangerous men."

He paused a minute. Alvin wondered what the punishment would be.

"And in the fifth place," continued Dad, his voice much lower and softer, "in the fifth place, your mother and I are the proudest parents in the whole wide world. We're proud that we have children who are so brave. And we're proud that we have children with imagination, who can use their heads to solve problems. Children, you'll never know how proud we are."

Dad cleared his throat and reached for his handkerchief. Mom was hugging the Pest.

In all his life, Alvin had never heard any words that made him feel so good. He felt as though he could lick the world. But there was something that still puzzled him, something he had to know before he could feel that the adventure was over.

"Dad, I still don't understand what was going on in that old house. After you brought us home and put us to bed last night, did you find out what those two men were trying to do? Who are they, anyway?"

"One of them is Mrs. Huntley's nephew, her only living relative. He's a lazy sort who tries to live on the work of other people. He brought one of his city friends with him, another shiftless character. They were going to split up the money."

"What money?"

"Old Mrs. Huntley's money. Remember the stories about all of her money? For years everyone believed she had it hidden in a paper sack somewhere in that old house. Her nephew had heard those stories. He and his pal figured they'd force her to tell where the money was, then split it up and disappear."

"But why didn't Mrs. Huntley want us to tell the police?"

"Because her nephew was her only relative. She couldn't bring herself to believe that he should be arrested, that he's completely bad. And in one way, she's right. You kids should always remember that no one is *completely* bad. We're all a mixture. In each of us there's a little of the 'good guy' and a little of the 'bad guy.' In his case, most of the bad shows through instead of the good. He should be locked up, of course, for trying what he did. But by the time we started talking to him at the station last night, he already was beginning to feel some shame. Perhaps, after he's punished, he'll turn out all right. Perhaps sooner or later the 'good guy' will start showing through instead of the bad."

Just then there was a knock at the door. Dad crossed

the room and opened it. A little man with a moustache was standing there. Behind him was a big man with a camera.

"I'm from the *Daily Bugle*," said the man with the moustache. "I just heard about the story down at the police station. We're mighty proud of our delivery boy. I wonder if I could talk to him and his sister."

Dad looked at Alvin and Daphne. He lifted his eyebrows.

"I think Shoie ought to be here," said Alvin. "Let's go find him."

Just as they walked through the front door, the Mighty Athlete came bounding down the street, did a back flip and landed at the bottom of the steps.

It was an exciting morning. The man with the camera lined up the children and started taking pictures.

Standing there in front of the camera, Shoie whispered out of the corner of his mouth, "I didn't even get bawled out."

"Neither did we," answered Alvin. "Well, hardly."

Then the man asked them all sorts of questions. All three of them had to tell the story again. At last the man turned to Daphne and said, "And what were you thinking about, little lady, while you were standing by that door with the bag of popcorn in your hand?"

"I was thinking," said the Pest, "I was thinking that I had the smartest brother in the whole world, and if he said his Automatic Man Trap would work, then it would work."

That touched off a whole batch of new questions about Alvin's inventions. The man with the moustache even sent the man with the camera upstairs to photograph Alvin's inventing bench.

A few minutes later, Mom suddenly shrieked in dismay. She had just noticed that Alvin was wearing a filthy pair of pants. She insisted that he change them.

"But the Pest has on her nightgown," complained Alvin.

The man with the moustache was making notes on a pad of paper. He looked up. "Is that what you call her? The Pest?"

Alvin paused for just a moment, looking down at his sister's upturned face. Her golden curls were shining in the sunlight. "No," he said. "No, this is my sister Daphne."

The Pest threw her arms around him and buried her face in his shirt.

By now the neighbors were gathering on the front lawn, trying to find out what had happened. A squad car pulled up at the curb, followed by Mr. McReynolds and three other firemen in the Chief's red car. Only once could Alvin ever remember seeing more people on the front lawn. That was the time he blew out the basement window with his chemistry set. But this time all the people were looking at him in admiration.

Finally the man with the moustache said, "Alvin, I talked to Mrs. Huntley at the hospital just before I came here. She's very grateful to you kids for what you did. She claims she has a lot of money hidden somewhere around that old house, but she's forgotten where it is. She says that if anyone finds it, she wants to give you kids five hundred dollars as a reward. If you get a

reward, Alvin, our readers will want to know what you plan to do with it."

The magnificent brain suddenly stripped gears. Money! *The money!* He'd forgotten all about the package of money hidden under the stone.

Alvin went racing down the street. The crowd, caught up in the excitement, ran after him. Inside the fence, Alvin looked back. It was a funny sight. Men and women were struggling across the fence, and while he watched, Mr. Peskin, who was inclined to be fat, got snagged on top of the fence, and it took three other men to get him down.

By the time Alvin had found the right stone and pulled out the box, the crowd had gathered in front of the old house. He reached in the box and pulled

out the sack. He dumped it upside down on the porch steps.

A gasp went up from the crowd.

"There's the money," announced Alvin. "There's the money those two men were trying to steal. Mrs. Huntley probably figured it would be safer outside the house, where her birds could watch it, than inside, where everyone thought it was."

Now there were a good many more questions. Finally the man with the moustache pushed his way up until he was standing in front of Alvin once more.

"You didn't answer my question, Alvin," he said. "What do you plan to do with the five-hundred-dollar reward?"

Alvin thought for a moment. Enough money to patent his Paper Slinger!

He looked up at the sky and saw a bird soaring overhead. The thought came into his mind that perhaps that bird up there was Mr. Huntley looking over his old house. It was at that instant that the magnificent brain went soaring into action again, soaring like the bird.

Someone tugged at his sleeve, and he heard the words, "reward money" again.

Alvin Fernald, Great Inventor, answered the question quite simply. "I've been doing some thinking about gravity," he said. "If we could get rid of gravity we could fly like a bird. I have an idea for a Super Magnetic Gravity Overcomer. I don't think Shoie and I and the — and Daphne — would take any money from old Mrs. Huntley. But if she wants to contribute something to science, she might want to buy some magnets and a few other things I'll need for my new Gravity Overcomer."

Shoie and the Pest looked at him. There was surprise in their eyes. There was admiration, too.

Alvin didn't notice it. His own eyes were getting glassy. "You see," he went on, analyzing the problem without even realizing he was giving words to his thoughts, "there are at least three ways to overcome gravity. One is with wings. Another is with balloons filled with gas. I prefer the third way. I plan to fasten those magnets. . . ."

ABOUT THE AUTHOR

Clifford Hicks is the father of three boys. In their home in a suburb of Chicago the boys have an "inventing bench" similar to Alvin's, and for a good many years their father has watched them dream up all sorts of interesting contraptions. While Mr. Hicks was writing this book, one son was developing a howitzer to shoot dried peas, using a mousetrap as a propellant. Another was working on an idea for a fireplace lighter. "You pulled a lever, which turned a wheel, which moved a special part from an Erector set, which rubbed a match against a piece of sandpaper and then stuck the lighted match into the fire. Clearly better than an ordinary match," says Mr. Hicks.

Mr. Hicks was born in Marshalltown, Iowa, and was graduated *cum laude* from Northwestern University with a Bachelor of Science degree. He is now assistant managing editor of a popular scientific and mechanical magazine. He has written free-lance fiction and non-fiction for magazines and is the author of FIRST BOY ON THE MOON.